A
HOUSE CALLED
PLEASANCE

A
HOUSE CALLED
PLEASANCE

Laura Conway,

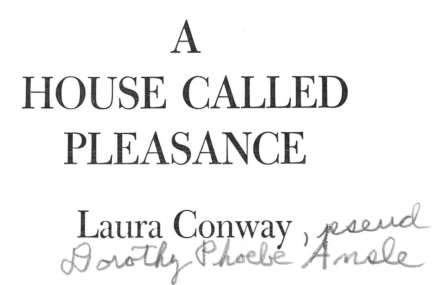

Dorothy Phoebe Ansle pseud

E.P. Dutton New York

PART ONE
1537

❋ CHAPTER 1 ❋

'It is a great honour,' said Lady Grenton, 'and your father and I pray you will prove worthy of it. Bestir yourself, Annis; there is no time for you to stand thus in a dream, staring out upon the courtyard. There is nothing to be seen. The messengers sent by His Majesty's grace are at supper, and their horses are in the stables.'

Annis Grenton, turning away from the window, broke in upon her stepmother's flustered talk, which being flustered was in itself extraordinary. As a rule, Lady Grenton was a coldly composed woman.

'Am I expected to ride all the way to Hampton?' Annis asked. 'Your ladyship well knows that I am an indifferent horsewoman.'

'You will go thence by coach. As it has not been used for long, it is now being scoured and polished. Oh, the pother there has been these last few hours, though had we been apprised earlier, all could have been arranged smoothly. But it is not, as your father says, for us to question His Majesty's command which requires you to make all speed to attend the Queen.'

Lady Grenton's irritation was as much with Annis as with the unexpected turn of events. There she stood; tall, fair, solid, contemplative and apparently not in the least excited or perturbed.

'It can be no more than a whim of the Queen's,' Annis said. 'If she has repented of it by the time I arrive, I may be sent home again.'

From the flicker of expression that passed across Lady Grenton's face, it was apparent that the same thought had occurred to her, and her next words admitted it.

'It is a time when any woman, even a Queen, has her whims, but that is not your concern or ours, who have only to obey. See that such a dismissal, if it should come about, is through no fault of yours, daughter.'

Annis stared, as well she might. It was the first time that the cold woman whom her father had married over four years ago had addressed her as 'daughter'. Her mother had been of humble origin and Lady Grenton, a wealthy squire's only daughter, was not the one to allow her to forget it.

At Pleasance, Annis's role was that of an unwanted dependant, though she was not a useless one, having been taught to spin and bake and to embroider. She was barely twelve when her mother died, and there had been two years of turmoil before Sir Lucian Grenton, her father, married again; years in which he lived wildly with dissolute companions, drinking and gaming, and his name became a local scandal.

In those years Annis ran wild. She was neglected and almost forgotten, and since then had been frequently told that she had good reason to be grateful to her stepmother who had rescued her from an existence which could but have ended in disaster.

Isabel Grenton had also rescued Sir Lucian. She was an orphan and an heiress, and at twenty-eight answerable only to herself. Her fortune had been used to pay his debts and to repair Pleasance which was in a sad state by the time Sir Lucian married her.

A cold, plain, resolute woman, Isabel had cast desirous eyes upon the still handsome rake, fifteen years her senior, and she had set herself to reform and to generally re-establish one whom had she been younger and with her parents alive, she would not have been allowed to marry; her task made the easier by the fact that Sir Lucian's health had declined, and that once snared he had lacked the strength to oppose her. For the past year he had been a semi-invalid, and it was Isabel who virtually managed the estate. Although a steward was employed, he was too much in awe of her to question any of her decisions.

Nowadays, there was small trace of the old Sir Lucian. He was entirely under the thumb of his capable wife. The outside world saw little of him; even his daughter saw little of him. Lady Grenton was a jealous woman, and there were occasions when her husband's glance lingered too fondly for her liking on his only child. Then she realized that he was recalling Annis's mother whose beauty had been locally famous. Only such great beauty, allied to spotless virtue could have brought about the marriage between Sir Lucian Grenton and the daughter of one who although he called himself yeoman, was little more than a labourer.

Annis lacked her mother's ethereal beauty but Lady Grenton, who remembered her husband's first wife, admitted that she was comely and that there was a likeness. She contrived that father and daughter were rarely together. That was not difficult, since Sir Lucian with his gout and other ailments now rarely left his room, and Annis was forbidden to enter it unless specifically sent there by her stepmother.

With the aid of a servant-girl whom she had trained to attend upon an invalid, Isabel acted as her husband's nurse. At one time she had also been his hostess, but their guests had been of her choosing; she had sedulously discouraged his former comrades. Now that he had sunk into invalidism, few called except the priest and the physician; yet the usual state was maintained. There were horses in the stables that Sir Lucian would never ride again; grooms to exercise them; a clutter of servants, and vast meals cooked in the big kitchens. Baking, brewing, preserving followed the usual ritual, but except for a dinner-party given twice a year, all entertaining had ceased.

The great house was kept in speckless order for the gratification of its mistress, who had boundless energy and sharp eyes to detect the smallest cobweb or trace of dust. For months, Sir Lucian had been scarcely so much as a figure-head, though his wife was punctilious in issuing orders as though directed by him.

Annis thought that he cared little now for what went on around him. She doubted if even this extraordinary command that she was to present herself at Hampton Court really stirred him. It was her stepmother who realized that she was incapable of riding the forty-odd miles to Hampton, even though the small cavalcade would stop for a night on the way. There was nothing for it but the coach, as it would not

7

be seemly for her to ride pillion.

The coach had not been used for years. Sir Lucian hated its gloomy interior and its springless discomfort and Lady Grenton was an intrepid horsewoman who despised Annis because she was scared of horses and became sick and dizzy when mounted upon one. But then, thought Annis resentfully, *she* had not been thrown from a horse when she was a child. Annis had, and for a time it was feared that her back was badly injured. The accident had left her with an horrific memory which persisted to this day; that arching curve through the air, the ground coming up to meet her, and afterwards the darkness and pain.

But there was also sweetness to recall. Her handsome, god-like father's concern for her, and her mother's petting. She had been made to feel her importance to them both, which was not always apparent, for they were sufficient to each other. There never had been a lady more loved by her lord, so Annis had been told by the one old servant who remained at Pleasance after Sir Lucian's second marriage. Lysbeth, now in her sixties, had been Sir Lucian's nurse and he refused to have her sent away. The others had all been dismissed. Isabel preferred to be served by those of her own choice, being jealous of those who remembered the first Lady Grenton with affection.

Well, and who could wonder at it? Annis asked herself with a sidelong glance at the plain, flat-bosomed woman. Her mother had had the best of her father; his second wife had taken possession when he was no more than a wreck of his former self; his fine constitution ruined by the incessant drinking bouts through which he had dulled his grief for the wife so dearly loved.

The spotted fever had taken her as it took so many, and Sir Lucian had raved and cursed because it had not also taken him. He had tended her with his own hands, though Annis had been shut away from her chamber, and the maids had been terrified to go near their mistress. Hushed whispers of her end had reached Annis's ears . . . the dreadful sight of her in those last days; her lovely face swollen and unrecognizable, her lips parched, her cracked voice rising in delirium. The fever had struck and had killed her in three days.

The Annis of eighteen vividly remembered the anguish of being twelve and motherless and of no comfort to the father who scarcely seemed to realize that she existed. And afterwards there had been chaos; the house filled with coarse-tongued men; the everlasting gambling and drinking and general disorder. Servants had come and gone. Miss Everley, Annis's governess, had left in tears, vowing that this was no establishment for a self-respecting woman of good breeding. Annis cared nothing. She had disliked the prim governess who kept her so closely at her books. A giggling, disrespectful young maid told Annis that Mr Tollard of Heppam Manor had one day seized upon Miss Everley as she was descending the stairs, and had forcibly kissed and cuddled her; he being in his cups, and even when sober a roistering blade with whom no respectable girl would trust herself for five minutes.

After that there had been nobody except old Lysbeth, groaning with her rheumatism, to care what happened to Annis. The other servants had been kind enough, and saw that she was well fed, but apart from that she had suffered neglect until Isabel became her stepmother. Then there were lessons again and rules and an orderly household, and her outgrown, shabby clothes were replaced by neat garments.

A great girl of fourteen she had been by then, and her appearance a scandal, so the new wife said, bidding Susan Partridge, who was appointed to look after her, to comb the snarls out of her thick, fair hair, and to burn her disreputable clothes.

But it was only today, within the last few hours, that Annis had come to think of Susan as her personal maid. Formerly, Lady Grenton would not have allowed her to suppose that she was of sufficient importance to possess one. But now she had said that as it was impossible for her to leave Sir Lucian in his poor state of health, and as Annis would be expected to have her own waiting-woman, she was thankful that she could trust Susan to accompany her to Hampton. Susan was a sensible young woman; there was nothing scatter-brained about her, nothing flighty. Annis, mindful of Susan's badly pock-marked face, and of her lumpy figure, thought it would have ill-suited her to be flighty.

9

'Susan is packing for you now,' said Lady Grenton, 'though I am mortified to send you away so ill-provided for. Leading such a quiet life here, you have not needed more than plain gowns, but there are silk and damask lengths which I have by me, and these shall go with you. Susan is skilled with her needle, and you will surely have spare hours in which you can help her to sew for you. There is also my blue velvet cloak and hood. These you shall have, and anything else suitable that I can find at such short notice. The Queen's grace has not considered these inconveniences . . .'

'Does it matter, madam? The Queen, so she writes in her letter, is shut away. She will see nobody but her ladies for the next few weeks.'

'I would not for your father's sake have them look down on you,' Lady Grenton said. 'He has told me to send you with a full purse. No doubt you will be able to purchase all that is necessary, but such matters take time . . .' She broke off and added in a voice that was as dazed as Annis's voice : 'It is the most curious thing that she has so set her heart on you, and for your companionship, so she writes. When she honoured us in the spring, I had thought there was little opportunity for her to notice you.'

'She bade me stay when I followed Lysbeth who took her supper tray to her. She was lonely, perhaps. She talked to me.'

Lady Grenton scoffed at that. 'How could she have been lonely, you foolish chit, when she had so many in her train and all with no thought but for her? The King would not have left her side had he not trusted those about her. Still, I allow she has a child-like manner – something simple and natural. It is said that for this the King loves her and the more dearly, comparing her to that flaunting other . . .'

The thoughts of both women were now centred on the event of over six months ago; an even more startling happening than that which had occurred today.

The King and his Court had been on a tour to Lincoln, and he with his escort had pressed ahead leaving the Queen to follow in her horse-drawn litter. At the beginning of the journey, until she tired, she had been riding her white mare beside him but then, though transferred to the litter, she still ached with weariness and she had commanded a messenger on a swift horse to speed onwards, bearing her message to the great house in Lincoln where the King and Queen and their entourage were expected, and where the King must have already arrived. She was forced to tarry, the Queen pleaded, and one of her ladies being a distant cousin of Lady Grenton whose home was nearby had suggested that there she might lodge for the night and make all speed in the morning to join His Majesty in Lincoln. She prayed that His Grace might pardon her weakness and grant his indulgence.

At Pleasance they were all thrown into confusion when the glittering cavalcade with the pale, half-fainting, Queen in its midst had passed up the avenue to the house. Annis, though she had no love for her stepmother, had been forced to admire her self-possession, the authority with which she acted. Greeting the Queen with a sweeping curtsy and fluent words of welcome, she had sent the servants flying to open up rooms, which because of her meticulous standards were ready for use at any time. The young Queen had seemed to marvel at her; she had been grateful and apologetic; seemingly unaware of the honour she conferred.

Annis, for all the grandeur of the Queen's raiment and the bleating of her attendants, had seen a girl of more simplicity of nature than herself; one who although she had been singled out for greatness, had not lost a gentleness which verged on timidity.

Her fatigue at first was pitiful. She had sighed with exhaustion as her ladies disrobed her, and sponged her face and hands with warm water. Supper was brought to her in the big guest-room, cheerful with the fire which leapt in the grate and alight with many candles. The finest, lavender-scented sheets had been spread on the great bed, and propped up against the pillows. There, Queen Jane in her fur-edged night-shift had reclined and smiled at Annis, younger by far than any of the ladies in her entourage.

She had sent them away to eat, to rest, though later as custom dictated one must return to sleep on the pallet at the foot of the bed. But until then ...

'Stay with me for a while,' the Queen had requested. 'Tell me about yourself and your life here. Your good father is sick, I am told, but surely he will soon recover in such peaceful, beautiful surroundings.'

She bade Annis draw a stool to the side of the bed, and while she ate sparingly of the food on her tray, she questioned her. Annis had not said that her life was far from happy. She knew better than that, but possibly the Queen had divined it, hearing that Lady Grenton was her stepmother and drawing Annis out to speak of her own mother. To one who evinced such sympathetic interest Annis had owned to a longing to see something of the world beyond her immediate environment. The nearest country town was ten miles away, and even to ride there and back was a rare event in her life. Once and once only had her father taken her to a fair there, and the memory of it was still vivid; the tumblers and acrobats, the booths where wool and cloth and household goods were on sale, and the crowds that had gathered round a poor, half-blind bear, which was tied to a stake, while dogs baited it. Annis had caught only a glimpse of this sport and had wanted to see no more.

'My father begged that treat for me,' she told the Queen. 'My stepmother was against it. She would not be seen there. It was not suitable, she said, for anyone above a farmer's wife, but I had done well at Latin and figures and my father wished to reward me.'

That treat had been given during the early months of Sir Lucian's second marriage, before Isabel had gained complete domination over him, but she had already changed Annis's appearance, and Sir Lucian had been fleetingly proud of his fair, comely daughter, verging on womanhood, and showing an aptitude for her studies. There was no resident governess, but a schoolmaster called three times a week to instruct her, while old Lysbeth with her needlework sat in the same room to chaperon her.

'Mine is so dull a life. It can but weary Your Grace to hear of it,' Annis had protested when the Queen continued to question her.

But, strangely, the Queen had seemed interested and as the food and wine revived her and she stretched her body in the soft bed, she had herself started to talk; she had told Annis something of the life at Court; describing the dancing and the minstrels playing; the tournaments and the pageants. The King, said Queen Jane, was a sweet singer beyond compare but for herself she had no more singing voice than the chirp of a sparrow. Annis, listening enthralled, confessed that she also, although her stepmother sang and played the virginals, was but a poor performer.

All the while they talked, the Queen's eyes were fixed on Annis's face; it was almost as though she could not draw away her gaze. Annis, in her respect, had not dared to stare as openly though she would have liked to. The Queen was pale with an icy pallor. She had large, doe-soft eyes and a sweet, small mouth. Her brown hair had a slight wave and was as soft as silk. Her slender hands looked almost transparent.

Queen Jane had kept Annis with her until the lady-in-waiting who was to sleep in her chamber made an apologetic appearance, and then she was dismissed, though with reluctance. The grand company departed early the next morning, and Annis had caught but a glimpse of the Queen, and only that because she was commanded to appear.

Bidding farewell to Lady Grenton, the Queen had said that she would wish to give both her hostess and her stepdaughter a keepsake. They had knelt before her, and she had pinned a pearl brooch to Lady Grenton's kerchief, and had fastened a gold chain about Annis's neck.

'His Majesty the King would desire you to have a remembrance of me,' she said, 'because of the kindness you have accorded me.'

Lady Grenton had protested that the honour of receiving the Queen was sufficient and Jane had smiled absently at her and gazing at Annis had said that one day they might meet again.

With a sigh of mingled relief and gratification Lady Grenton had watched the cavalcade depart. The Queen, much refreshed and no longer with dark shadows beneath her eyes, had been mounted on her white mare; the horse-drawn litter, now unoccupied, following at the rear of the procession.

The visit was talked of for many a long day and Lady Grenton sorely regretted that Sir Lucian had been too ill to rise from his bed to act as host. Nothing had seemed more improbable to Annis than that the Queen would give her another thought; but it seemed that she had. Without warning, three horsemen in the royal livery had arrived at Pleasance, bearing a letter written in the Queen's own hand, desiring her company at Hampton Court during the last weeks of her pregnancy. Annis had been stunned, and Lady Grenton at first incredulous. Now the latter said : 'The Queen must have known, or at least strongly suspected that it was so with her, even last April. Did she hint at that, to you?'

Annis shook her head : 'I cannot remember that she did – at least, except for the green figs. She said how strange it was that in the ordinary way she had no fancy for these, but that now she had a craving for them. None had been preserved from last summer, as your ladyship will remember it was a bad year for them, and the Queen said the King had promised to send messages to France for the first that ripened there. I told her we had plum and quince preserve, but she had no wish to try either.'

'If you had told me that, I should have known at once what ailed her,' said Lady Grenton. 'I have heard often enough of these erratic fancies. I only wish . . .'

She gazed before her with an abstracted expression, conscious, Annis supposed, of her own childlessness. She realized with satisfaction that it was unlikely she would have stepbrothers or sisters. This dominating woman who had reformed a husband, disciplined a stepdaughter and brought a country estate into such order that they were self-provisioned, with their own cattle and horses bred for purchase, had failed to produce an heir. Annis had heard the gossip of the upper servants, who now sometimes eyed her with respect as the heiress who would inherit all when her father died. Lady Grenton had poured her own wealth into the estate, or so she was fond of saying, but on marriage a woman's fortune became her husband's. No doubt, thought Annis, a jointure had been secured to her, but when she married and was mistress here, her stepmother would retire to the Dower House.

It was an intoxicating thought, though it was not one upon which she cared to dwell. She loved her father and hoped he would live for many years, though not that he would sire a half-brother to displace her. When she at last came into her own, thought Annis grandly, she would be just to her step-mother, and treat her generously, little though she liked her.

She hoped that before then a suitable match would have been made for her. There had been talk before her mother's death but nothing actually settled. Young Gerard Pommard was sixteen years to her twelve; neither of them were then too young for a formal betrothal, and his family and the Grenton family had been friends for generations. The Pom-mard estate was the nearest of any consequence, and as Gerard was the youngest of five brothers it would have been a good marriage for him. But all negotiations ceased when Sir Lucian started on a course of dissipation and it was known that he was rapidly squandering the family revenues. Young Gerard had been sent abroad to complete his education, and shortly before Sir Lucian's second marriage, he had married a French girl somewhat older than himself but with a lavish dowry.

Even at fourteen, Annis had been miserably humiliated.

It was almost as though Lady Grenton guessed the thought that had flashed through her stepdaughter's mind, for she said: 'It may be that if the Queen is pleased with you and you remain with her after the birth of the prince, with whom it is hoped she will be blessed, that some suitable alliance can be considered. This would have more preoccupied me but for your father's ill-health. You are eighteen, and it is fully time you were wed. His health has somewhat improved of late, so I may venture to put the matter before him. It would be difficult to arrange a marriage for you locally, but as the Queen is inclined to interest herself in you – and as thanks to my efforts there will be a provision for you . . .' Lady Grenton broke off, and then ended abruptly: 'You are not ill-looking, as well I dare say as many of those attached to the Court.'

'You think I may meet someone who will want to marry me while I am at Hampton?' asked Annis bluntly. 'To me it seems unlikely, for although the Queen may favour me I shall be an outsider there. Why does your ladyship say that it would be especially difficult for a match to be made for me locally? There was talk of it years ago.'

'I doubt if it was more than talk,' Lady Grenton returned snubbingly. 'Your father was too optimistic. I heard it discussed myself, and I believe Lord Pommard, having been his friend for many years, was loth to reject his daughter as a possible wife for a son of his. However that may be, he took the first opportunity of abandoning such a tentative suggestion, and this was not only because of the wildness into which your poor father plunged.'

'What other reasons could there be to make me – unacceptable?' Annis demanded.

'Surely it is unnecessary to ask. You are aware of your mother's status. You owe your breeding to your father, not to her whose low origin will in this neighbourhood be set against your other advantages. My hope is that in London it will be thought of small importance; that is to say if the Queen's favour continues, and if you conduct yourself as a lady of quality. Do not, I pray you, Annis, tighten your lips in that unbecoming manner, or so narrow your eyes to slits. I speak only for your own good, and am telling you nothing that you do not already know.'

Unable to speak for the anger which had welled up in her heart, Annis turned away. The impatience and dislike which she could usually suppress had quickened to hatred. At last she found voice to say: 'My father loved my mother. She was good and beautiful.'

'Certainly she was, but she was also the daughter of one who was little but a herdsman. She was illiterate and could barely write her own name; and when your father married her he settled money on her indigent family and had them shipped to Ireland, from whence I believe they originally came. Mercifully, nobody has heard of them since. Your mother's face was her fortune. Let us hope that you, who are so much better schooled, will do as well for yourself. Now we have talked for long enough, and if you are to leave here tomorrow there is little time to do all that must be done. In your state of nervous excitement, which I allow is but natural, it is certain that most of the preparations for your departure will fall upon me.'

With these words Lady Grenton sailed from the room. Annis so far forgot herself, or so far reverted to the low status of her maternal ancestors as to plant her hands on her hips and stick out her tongue at her stepmother's retreating figure.

CHAPTER 2

Throughout the first days at Hampton Court, Annis was gloomily aware that if her looks were her fortune, they would not take her far. By the standards of the maids of honour, and even those of lower degree, she was dowdy and almost uncouth.

On arrival she had been greeted civilly enough by two of the older ladies whom she had met the previous spring at her own home. They, she was told, had been instructed by the Queen's grace to see that she was welcomed and lodged in comfort. The Queen would not see her until the following morning. Her Majesty was sure that the traveller would be weary, and had herself been afflicted all day with the tooth-ache. That was a complaint from which she had suffered much of late.

Annis was thankful for the respite for on the rough roads, in the springless coach which was little more than a bedizened cart with curtains, she had had such a shaking that she felt bruised from head to foot.

Moreover, no sooner was she beyond sight of Pleasance than homesickness set in, and that had gathered strength throughout the journey. *En route* they had stopped for a night at an inn where Annis especially was miserably uncomfortable, tormented by the fleas which commonly infested floors strewn with infrequently changed rushes. For most of the night she had been kept awake, madly scratching at the inflamed and itching lumps which appeared on her fair skin. Susan was less afflicted and could have slept but that Annis waked her. Her hide, she said cheerfully, was harder and less toothsome to the ravenous insects. Finally, such were Annis's complaints that Susan had descended the stairs to the kitchen, where the inn servants were sprawled sleeping on the floor. There she found some vinegar and returned with it, soaking a towel with which she had sponged her young mistress. This eased the torment, but Annis was mortified by the stink of vinegar which still hung about her even when she arrived at Hampton; moreover, there were unsightly blotches on her cheeks and arms. Amused and supercilious gazes had been fixed upon them.

Grudgingly, she had reflected approvingly upon Lady Grenton's housewifely care. There were no rush-strewn floors at Pleasance. Her stepmother insisted on stone and wood, well scrubbed with the soap which was a home produce. At Hampton Court, grand though it was, Annis thought it probable that the servants were less well-trained. Within forty-eight hours Susan had dusted and scoured the two rooms allotted to them, though she had not been told that it was her duty to keep them in order.

As soon as possible, she started to fashion a gown for Annis from the roll of plum-coloured damask which Lady Grenton had bestowed on her. Her best dress, which at Pleasance was worn only for Sunday church-going, had been donned on her first day at Hampton in readiness for the Queen's summons. That occurred shortly before noon.

The Queen's lying-in was not expected for a month or possibly longer, but it was the custom for royal females to thus seclude themselves at the end of pregnancy, and the Queen would now be seen by none save the King, her physicians, and her ladies until after the birth of her child. However much she might long for exercise in the fresh air this would be denied her, though in theory every wish must be promptly gratified.

Queen Jane, well aware of what was expected of her, made no such request and in fact was frightened that fresh air, even here at Hampton Court, might carry on it the seeds of the dreaded plague that periodically ravaged the city.

Escorted to the royal suite, Annis found that the Queen was not alone. Sitting near to her on a low stool was a fragile-looking young woman, small of stature and with heavy-lidded dark eyes. The Queen held out her hand to Annis, who knelt to kiss it, and she was then told that the Queen's companion was the Lady Mary, the King's elder daughter, and once again she put her lips to an outstretched hand.

'It was good of you to come so promptly,' the Queen said, 'although it is my hope that it will pleasure you to keep me company, it was chiefly for my own sake that I sent for you. All my dreams of late, as I have been telling the Lady Mary, have been of cream and roses and the country; and when I first saw you last April that is of what you made me think; cream, roses, honey. Again and again, as though it was a portent, I have felt that I should be the better for having you near me. Is she not a picture of health, Mary? So strong, so fair, as though no disease could put a finger on her; as though she could well be a talisman for me?'

Mary, the daughter of the deposed and dead Katherine of Aragon, gazed seriously at Annis and as seriously agreed, but Annis's heart took a downward plunge. The fact that she had been remembered and was here was now explained; it was as she had half-feared – nothing but the sick fancy of a pregnant woman, though the fantasy that the near presence of abundant rude health would be a safeguard had certainly not occurred to her. In such an odd freak of the imagination Annis had no belief. If she was noticeably strong and flourishing it was because she had led a secluded country life unfamiliar to great ladies. Both the Queen and the Lady Mary looked as though a puff of wind might seriously injure them, but one could not transmit such health.

The Queen's peculiar pallor was part of her beauty, and although she was now big with child that did not make her look the less fragile. Annis pitied her, and it passed through her mind to wonder that the King, who so longed for a male heir, had wed three women who according to current gossip could none of them be accounted robust. Although she knew nothing whatever of Court life, the King's doings, and especially his matrimonial misfortunes, were discussed in every town and village of his realm. Annis, though only a child at the time, had heard the talk about his divorce from Queen Katherine who had borne several children either still-born or too weak to survive infancy. The Lady Mary, who might no longer be called Princess because the King's marriage to

Queen Katherine had been declared null and void, was the one living child of that union. Since then there had been another dead son by the witch-Queen, Anne Boleyn, but there was her child still living, the little Lady Elizabeth.

Annis had had only a distorted knowledge of the witch-Queen's alleged crimes, for these were considered too foul for mention in a young girl's hearing, but during the flea-tormented night at the inn Susan Partridge and she had gossiped and speculated, and Susan being beyond range of Lady Grenton's censure had revealed many lurid details.

Anne Boleyn, she told Annis, had betrayed the King, not only with one gallant but with several and – a terrible and loathsome sin – one of these had been her own brother. Darkly beautiful though she was, she had had a deformed hand; five fingers on it instead of four – sure sign that she was a witch, and that she had captured the King by putting a spell upon him. It was said that although Queen Katherine was deposed, the witch-Queen grudged her her very life. She had bribed villains to poison the poor creature, and it was only through the intervention of heaven that the Lady Mary had escaped the same fate.

But when Susan spoke of Anne Boleyn's execution, horror veered to admiration, for she had shown great bravery and had gone unfalteringly to her death. The executioner from France had been brought from thence to despatch her with his great sword. It had whistled through the air, and at one stroke . . .

The shuddering Annis had listened breathlessly, almost forgetting the maddening irritation of her flea-bites and the stench of the vinegar.

Now she gazed with a new, secret fascination at Queen Jane who had succeeded the wicked Anne Boleyn. Was it good fortune or ill that when she was Lady Jane Seymour, and one of Anne's maids of honour, the King's fancy had fallen upon her? Even before the visit last April, Annis had heard much of her virtue, her purity, and it was not difficult to believe that this had held the amorous Henry at bay. She *looked* good, thought Annis, but she had been right when she judged the Queen to have a simple nature. Who that was otherwise than simple would think the close companionship of one who reminded her of cream, roses and honey could affect her own health?

Annis silently agreed with the Lady Mary when she now said: 'Dear Jane, you need no such talisman. If you will be the calmer and happier for Annis's presence, then that is well and none will grudge it to you, but in these last weeks and in your travail you will be in God's protection, in Our Lady's protection, and that is your safety.'

'I do not doubt it,' said the Queen, and swiftly crossed herself with a slender, jewelled hand. 'I beseech Our Lady to intercede for me, that I may give the King's grace the fine, strong son for whom he longs.' But even as she spoke, her great eyes rested hauntingly on Annis's round face, flushed beneath the faint sun-tan.

The Lady Mary rose. Although she was short, she moved with much grace and dignity. Her sapphire velvet gown fell in heavy folds from her narrow waist; a gold chain from which a cross of pearls depended was slung from her neck.

'She will hear. She never fails to hear.' Mary, bending, kissed the Queen's hand and then her brow. 'You are so good, Jane, so kind; no harm will befall you.'

With a gracious smile for Annis the King's daughter left them alone together. As the door closed upon her, the Queen said: 'She has such faith. The Lady Mary has always been my dear friend, and so was her poor mother. I was one of her maidens, and never did I receive a harsh word from her. Then, when she died, I was brought to the Court of the late Queen Anne, and she . . .'

The Queen broke off, shivering slightly. 'Sit near to me,' she commanded. 'Give me your hand to hold. That was what I wanted to do when I first saw you in the spring. You smoothed the sheet above me, and for an instant you touched me and it was as though strength flowed into me. I was not then sure that I had conceived – I had had hope once before that was misplaced, and was afraid it might be so again. I had not told the King, or he would not have permitted me to undertake the journey, which was only for the sake of the Lincoln pageant that was to honour our marriage.'

Annis felt the other's too thin fingers on hers which were plump and smooth. Her stepmother, through a sense of fitness, never allowed her to attempt any rough work. Once more the Queen sighed, though now it was with contentment. 'There is the same strength,' she murmured. 'It will not harm you to give me a part of it . . . it will rob you of nothing.'

'If I could, I would give Your Grace all the strength that is in me,' said Annis, and perhaps for the moment she meant it.

'But then,' said the Queen smiling at her fantasy, 'you would be weaker than I; you would be but a wraith, and there are wraiths enough in this old palace. I have no wish to evoke another.'

As Annis gazed at her with her hand held fast, it seemed to her that the Queen's pallor deepened; or was that because the circles beneath her eyes were suddenly darker? She moved restlessly in her padded, high-backed chair, within the softness of the sable robe that enwrapped her.

'*She* is here, too often here,' the Queen whispered, and glanced uneasily around the room. 'She hates me, though I vow I had no thought of harming her; and wished her no ill. I would have saved her had that been possible, but Anne Boleyn should know better than any other that the King's grace is not to be denied.'

A chill crept over Annis as she listened to the wandering words. The hand which clutched hers was fever hot, but after a while it cooled and the Queen, twisting her swollen body into a more comfortable position, closed her eyes and said peacefully: 'I feel better already for your nearness. Do not leave me if I drowse for a while.'

Her eyes closed and there was silence. Annis, from where she sat, could gaze from the window upon the autumn gardens. Rain had started to fall and the room darkened. One of the Queen's ladies came in softly, and smiled with pleasure to see her mistress so peacefully asleep.

'It is well,' said the newcomer, 'for the Queen has slept little of late. Do not move, girl; stay with her for her comfort.'

Cramped, and becoming minute by minute more uncomfortable on the low stool, Annis did not dare to disobey, but in that darkening room she was glad of the presence of the elderly lady, who with her embroidery frame sat close to

22

the window in order that the light might fall upon it.

The Queen's rambling words haunted Annis, and she sensed with foreboding that it would not be the last time she would hear such words.

On being summoned to Hampton, she had been elated and had hoped that she might find favour and perhaps stay at Court for years, favoured and smiled upon by the Queen; but now she felt that a month would be too long, and that once the Queen was safely delivered, she would pray to be allowed to return to Pleasance. Better by far the dullness there and the reciprocated dislike of Lady Grenton than this haunted magnificence and the fear of the King, who in a moment's anger or distrust could cause one's head to fall tumbling from one's body.

✳ CHAPTER 3 ✳

First impressions were later revised, for at Hampton Court Palace it was not all gloom. The Queen might be shut away in her suite, but there was gaiety amongst those who were not required to wait on her.

The great palace housed many courtiers who were there partly to beguile the King, partly to await the festivities which would follow the news of the Queen's safe delivery. Most of them were adepts at whiling away the time both for themselves and the impatient monarch.

There were also young women in plenty, and older ones to frown and rebuke if they showed undue forwardness towards any particular young man. In theory at least, the Queen's maids of honour and the younger waiting-women were strictly chaperoned. Many of the courtiers who held nebulous appointments were as gay as peacocks in their satin doublets and bright silk hose. Short velvet capes caught by jewelled brooches depended from their shoulders. Vividly-coloured feathers waved in their caps.

Annis, from a secluded alcove, and in her awkward sense of being an outsider glad to be unobserved, would watch them as they came and went, clustering in small groups, laughing and talking. The ladies mingled with them, though there were too many duennas around forbidding easy companionship. But that they met and courted in secret Annis did not doubt; even if modest, downward glances and a reserve of manner denoted otherwise.

On the whole, the ladies of the Court were less brilliant in appearance than were the men. Queen Jane, even when in health, was of a different type from the flamboyant Anne Boleyn and Anne's particular style, which had once been copied, had fallen into disrepute. The Lady Mary, now once more in favour with her royal father, was the social leader while the Queen was confined to her apartments. Mary invariably wore dark, majestic garments, and in general her manner was quiet and withdrawn, there being only rare occasions when she laughed or even smiled.

Early in her sojourn at the palace, Annis was presented to the King. One morning she was with the Queen in her boudoir when he strode in, and Annis got to her feet with haste, her genuflexion bringing her almost to the ground. Jane attempted to rise but that the King would not allow. Gently pushing her back into her chair, he tenderly kissed her, calling her his sweeting and his precious blessing.

The two other ladies who were present in addition to Annis, gazed up at him from their knees as they might have gazed at the sun, and indeed, although Henry Tudor was now in his late forties he still radiated power and vitality. Tall and portly with a broad, red face, in which by reason of its fleshiness, his eyes and mouth both appeared to be too small, his majesty was such that Annis was awed. Sky-blue and gold embroidery could have had a ludicrous effect on a lesser man but Henry, for all his girth and his porcine type of countenance, was never ludicrous.

Annis thought him terrifying and wondered at the Queen. How could this nervous, gentle young woman endure such a lover? It had been said that at one time Anne Boleyn had possessed great power over him, but Anne had been a witch, therefore power, until her spells withered and failed, must have been natural to her. Jane made no such impact; to Annis it was as though she had been sacrificed to a monster.

A genial monster, however, for Jane was now speaking of her, and the King turned his eyes upon her as she knelt there. Sitting beside his wife, with his left hand fondling her, the King stretched out his right to Annis as he bade the two other ladies to rise and be seated. With trepidation her lips touched a fat, be-ringed finger.

'So this is the Talisman,' the King said, and with his hand swerving to Annis's wrist, he raised her to her feet.

He laughed indulgently, and the Queen said: 'It can be nothing more than a foolishness in your eyes, my lord, and for that it is the more gracious of you to humour me.'

'I would humour you to the extent of bringing twenty such to Court, if you believed they could all give you a measure of their strength,' said Henry. 'But in sooth, now that I see this maiden, I am not so incredulous, for she is as you say of the good earth, which nourishes so many health-giving plants Roses and cream and honey, as you described her, and that was not too much. Such a bloom is unusual with our Court beauties.'

Annis, standing before him with drooping head, was blushing deeply, and she was more scared than she had ever been in her life. The frightful thought struck her that if the King did actually admire her, if he fixed his roving eye seriously upon her, it might well bring her to shame and grief; for as the Queen had said, who could dare deny him?

Her fear, however, was unwarranted. For once in his amorous life Henry, who in some ways had an uncomplicated mentality, was not interested in women. His sole purpose was to so pacify and content the Queen that she would have an easy and successful labour and present him with the strong man-child he was assured she was carrying.

Although he now detested the memory of Anne Boleyn, there were moments when he remembered with guilt that she might have borne a live son had he treated her with more consideration. Her last babe had possibly been born dead because of his unkindness. He had wearied of her by then, and was already enamoured of Jane Seymour. Anne, fearless to the last, had blamed him because her child was still-born, thus bringing down additional fury upon her head.

Jane should have no such cause for spleen. He was devoted

25

to her; her wifely submission was sweet to him, and the only occasion when there had been harsh words from him was when she pleaded for his daughter Mary, and even for the little Elizabeth. She wanted them both to be at Court with her, not kept in rural seclusion at Hunsdon, and the King, at first, had not been prepared to have them about him. Mary was in disgrace because she refused to avow that his marriage to her mother had been no true marriage and the three-year-old Elizabeth, although she resembled him, had also a fugitive likeness to Anne which was distasteful to him.

Jane had entreated him with tears, but in vain, until her pregnancy was established and then he had been unable to refuse her anything. He had promised that the girl of twenty-one, and the child of three should both be at Hampton Court Palace before her own child was born, and now that they were it did his heart good, so he told himself, to witness Jane's kindness to them.

She had always been attached to Mary, and it made no difference to her that the little Elizabeth's mother had been Anne Boleyn, though Anne and Jane had been on bad terms, and at the last Anne had raved at her, accusing her of every treachery.

Jane loved children, and Elizabeth was responsive to affection. Jane petted her and so did Mary, who was sufficiently magnanimous to overlook all that she and her mother had suffered through Anne. That wretched woman on the eve of her execution had sent Mary a message, begging her to be good to her little half-sister; and Mary, though stubborn and proud, had heeded that last entreaty.

Annis marvelled at the unity there now was between the various members of the royal family. The Lady Mary would forget her dignity to romp with the little half-sister, and the King and Queen would look on with smiling pleasure.

Sometimes there was music in the Queen's chamber. The Lady Mary would play the virginals, and the King would sing. He had a fine voice and many of the songs were of his own composing, both verses and music. Again on some days they would play cards, and as they were gambling card games, a considerable amount of money changed hands. The Lady Mary who loved to play, would sit tense and excited with spots of deep rose in her usually pale cheeks. If she won she was elated; if she lost the King would laugh his deep laugh and put out his hand for her empty purse that he might fill it again.

Always Annis was the onlooker, sitting near to the Queen, who often put out her hand to rest it on hers or upon her knee. Nobody was jealous of Annis, for all realized that her position at Court was but temporary. She was no more than the fancy of the Queen's pregnancy, and when once the child was born she would be sent home and thereafter forgotten.

Annis understood this general attitude and silently resented it. In order to warn Lady Grenton, she wrote to her to say that it was likely she would be at Pleasance again before the end of October, but she had not explained that the Queen's need of her was only a superstitious need. More than once Jane told Annis that she had but borrowed her for a while and would not for the world have her turned into an artificial Court lady.

Now that Annis was more familiar with the girls of her own age who had a permanent position at Court, and now that Susan had made new silk gowns for her in which she was sure that she looked as well as any of the others, she envied none of them.

By this time she knew something of the art of flirtation, and had been flattered by the passing admiration of various presentable young men. There had been a sonnet or two written to her; for in view of the Queen's favour, it would have seemed ungallant not to echo her approval. It was well known that the Queen compared her to cream and roses and honey, and the description was thought appropriate; but her country ruddiness was unfashionable, and none of these attractive males of a different world from hers endeavoured to lure her into a love affair. Annis was glad of it, for that was what her stepmother hoped for – a marriage which would take her stepdaughter far away and would rid her of further responsibility. She could not and would not be permanently separated from Pleasance. The thought of it tore her heart.

So it was, until fate brought her face to face with Nicholas Colton.

27

❋ CHAPTER 4 ❋

In the last week of September the Queen was in better health than she had been for some months. She slept more soundly, though as a rule not until after midnight. Annis, who was required to sit by her bed, often with the thin fingers twined in hers, would be half-stupefied with drowsiness and stifling her yawns. Not until the Queen slept was she free to disengage herself, to warn the lady in attendance who dozed on the pallet at the foot of her bed, and then to tip-toe softly from the royal suite and through the corridors to her own room.

In this stealthy withdrawal, she passed the door of the King's apartment, and sometimes she would hear him snoring, and think that the disgusting sound was very little different from the grunting of the satisfied pigs at Pleasance when they slept on full stomachs.

One evening when the Queen was more restless than usual, she asked Annis if she was capable of reading aloud, and at the note of doubt in her voice, Annis was glad to be able to say that that had been considered an important part of her education. At least, she thought, nobody could say of her that she was illiterate, and hated Lady Grenton again because of the accusation hurled at her mother.

Then she should read aloud to her, the Queen said, and asked if she had any acquaintance with the works of Chaucer or Cicero. There should be translations of Cicero on the bookshelf in the boudoir, or perhaps something lighter and more amusing would make a better lullaby – *Aesop's Fables* for instance.

Annis went in search of the book but could not discover it, and the Queen then said there must be a copy in the library which was at some distance from her suite but not hard to find. In the corridors candles burnt all night in their sconces, but Annis had better take another to give her additional light.

More than once she had lost her way in the winding passages, and in rooms which led through one another, but she listened attentively to the Queen's instructions which were clear enough, and only hoped she would not meet some amorous gallant on her way, though she would have defended herself stoutly had there been the necessity.

But on this occasion she met nobody as she went swiftly through deserted rooms and passages. From far away she could hear the strains of music and supposed, that as so often, there was dancing in the great hall.

Presently she was in a book-lined passage, and rightly supposed this to be an overflow of the library proper. A door at the end of it was ajar, and when she pushed it wide open, she saw a room ruddy from the wood-fire in the grate, and bright with many lighted candles. There were books lining the walls; she had never seen so many books before, and at a large table a man sat writing. His quill pen moved slowly across the sheet of parchment, his dark hair, worn rather long, fell over his eyes, and occasionally he put up his hand to brush it back. He was young and slender and of considerable good looks. Annis watched him with a curiously disturbed sensation. He was a stranger to her, and different from any of the courtiers she had met here; more soberly clad and with that in his expression which was earnest and profound.

Then he looked up and saw her standing there with the candlestick in her hand, and he stared at her as though she were a vision rather than an ordinary young woman.

'Is not this the library?' asked Annis. 'I am here to find a certain book for the Queen's grace.'

If there was a spell, it broke as she spoke. The young man rose to his feet and bowed. He said : 'At first – for a moment – I thought you were a ghost.'

'Are there such here? Oh dear, I hope not.'

Annis glanced around her so fearfully that he smiled as he answered : 'Sometimes I have almost thought so, but I am glad you are not one. You are one of Her Majesty's maidens, perhaps, as you are on an errand for her? A newcomer? You must be. I have seen most of her ladies from time to time. Not that they ever cross this threshold, but . . .'

'I am not exactly one of the Queen's maids. I am not precisely anything,' said Annis foolishly.

29

'An incarnation of Demeter, possibly.' And then as Annis looked puzzled : 'You have probably heard of her by her more usual title of Ceres.'

'The Goddess of Plenty – the Earth Mother, but I . . .'

'Demeter, though a matron, must once have been a girl; fair and peach-cheeked. One cannot believe that Proserpina, her daughter, having bitten into the pomegranate, was from thenceforth anything but dark and sallow.'

For once somebody other than Queen Jane was complimenting her on her good looks! Annis might think she was more nearly beautiful than many of the maids of honour, but she envied them their slender grace; their delicate hands and feet, and their faces which although seldom beautiful, had an aristocratic quality typified by heavy-lidded eyes, small mouths and long noses. Sometimes she had thought that the resemblance between the Court ladies was such that they could have been related by blood, and indeed they often were, for there was much inter-marriage in high circles.

'Tell me your name,' coaxed the young man, 'and I will tell you mine.'

'It is Annis Grenton. I am only to be here for a few weeks.'

'I am Nicholas Colton, and it is possible that the few weeks will also apply to me. You seem to be half-frightened of me, Demeter, and poised for flight.'

'Indeed I am not frightened. It takes much to frighten me, but I cannot delay. The Queen sent me for a book to enable her to sleep. I am to read it to her.'

'A particular book? Tell me, and I will search the shelves for it. Then, as the Queen's grace must not be kept waiting, I will not detain you; asking only that you will agree to meet me again. Shall it be tomorrow? Whatever your duties they cannot occupy you for every hour of the day, and I will accommodate my time to yours.'

Annis had no wish to deny him. She said : 'I am free in the mornings, when the Queen is refreshed by sleep and does not need me. Then she dismisses me while the King is visiting her, and afterwards she has the Lady Mary with whom she generally desires to be alone. I am sent out to take the air unless it rains. The Queen is concerned that I should not lose my colour or my freshness by being kept too long in her rooms with the closed windows.'

She spoke rapidly and with some incoherence, for she was eager to press into these few minutes all the information she could give him. Nicholas, whose eyes never left her face, said calmly : 'If it is wet, I will wait for you in the picture gallery; if it is fine I will be in the yew garden. Do not fear, we can find some place in which we can talk alone. Often I work all day here undisturbed, but as there is right of entry it is not secure. Now tell me the title of the book you require and I will search for it.'

On being told that this was *Aesop's Fables*, Nicholas Colton drew forward a short set of steps with a leather-covered seat on the top rung. 'There is,' he said, 'a copy here on the highest shelf. Caxton's translation and with wondrous illustrated plates.'

He was so tall that although the shelf was high it was only necessary for him to mount three steps to reach it. He took down the large, calf-bound volume and put it into her hands. When their fingers touched, a tremor shot through her, and she was loth to tear away her gaze from his thin, dark-skinned face. It seemed to her to be unlike any other mortal face with its finely chiselled features and velvet eyes.

'I will walk with you to the entrance of the Queen's suite,' Nicholas said. 'To be alone in these passages at night, which are cut off from the main corridor, can be as hazardous as walking the streets without an escort. Were you not in fear?'

'No. I thought it unlikely I should meet anybody, and who would dare to molest one who is under the Queen's special protection? When I first arrived here, a stranger, she put a ring of hers on my finger, and bade me to show it to anyone who might – might pursue me. The Queen said that once that was seen, nobody would dare for fear of the King's wrath. Unless,' added Annis, 'I were willing.'

'And have you been?' Nicholas asked.

She shook her head. 'I have suffered no temptation. I think it is realized that I am here for a purpose, almost a dedication.'

'You must explain about that to me tomorrow,' said Nicholas, and as he left her outside the door to the Queen's suite, he raised her hand to his lips.

❋ CHAPTER 5 ❋

After this, there was not a day upon which Nicholas and Annis did not contrive to meet, if only for a short while. They fully confided in each other.

Annis told him of her happy childhood which had ended so abruptly when she was twelve years old, and of her dislike of her stepmother. She described Queen Jane's unexpected short stay at Pleasance, and the surprising summons which had brought her to Hampton Court. In return, Nicholas told her that he was the nephew of the Hampton Court Palace librarian for whom the King had a genuine affection, being as great a lover of fine books as he was of music, and approving of any who shared such a love.

Nicholas's uncle had fallen ill a few weeks previously, and was now at his London home where he was being nursed through an attack of jaundice. Nicholas was the orphan son of his sister, who had made a poor and unworthy marriage, and he had been educated by his uncle to become a schoolmaster. He had had three appointments, Nicholas told Annis, and was actually engaged upon a memoir of the reign of Richard II. In this ambition he was encouraged by his uncle, and the King having heard of it had shown a gracious interest. It had been a simple matter for his uncle when he fell ill to arrange for Nicholas to act as his deputy until he recovered. That was why he had told Annis he did not expect to be at the palace for longer than a few weeks.

'I would not care to be here for ever,' he said, 'but for a short time it is an interesting experience and one which I shall often recall. The more often now and with tenderness.'

'But why speak as though it must be part of your past?' Annis remonstrated, for by this time they had known each other for over a week, and had fallen in love.

'Will it not be?' Nicholas fixed her with his dark eyes. 'What chance have we? I am without fortune and you are under-age and would never be allowed to marry me.'

'We are young. Conditions change,' pleaded Annis, 'and I shall not be dowerless. My father has had no children by his second marriage, and however much my stepmother dislikes me, she cannot prevent me from inheriting Pleasance. There can be no more beautiful house in the whole of England. We could both be happy there. I, managing it as my stepmother does, and you, writing your book and other books too when this is finished. Would not that be a life to content you?'

'It would content me if it were a certainty,' said Nicholas with a shrug and a smile. 'But there is none such. Your father is not an old man, and although he is sickly he may live for years, and surely, even for me, you would not grudge him a day of his life.'

'I could not. I love him. His death would be a great grief to me, but I think if I were to tell him about us, he would want to help us. Why not? Even my stepmother has said that I shall have a dowry.'

'If you make a good marriage, but not a marriage to such as I, who dowry or not, might well bring you to want. My sweet love, when you leave here you must forget about me.'

'How can you say that if you truly love me?' Annis reproached. 'But perhaps you do not. Perhaps because I have been truthful and told you about my mother's lowly birth, which means that nobody of quality within fifty miles or more of Pleasance will offer for me, you too would hesitate to wed me.'

'You know that is not so, Annis. If I were told that I had fifteen years of life ahead of me I would gladly surrender ten of them could I be sure of having the remaining five with you.'

It was as pretty a speech, thought Annis, as any gallant could have turned, though the serious, learnèd Nicholas was no gallant. She glowed because she was loved by one so clever and in her eyes so beautiful. She refused to believe that there was any insuperable bar to their future happiness, and with sudden fresh hope she said: 'When the Queen's grace has her babe in her arms, she will be grateful to me, for although it is nothing but a fantasy, it is surpassing real to her and she will believe that she drew strength from me. For that she will intercede for us with my stepmother, or she will entreat the King to command my father to consent. The King will not refuse her if she gives him his son. Even as of now he loves her tenderly, but then his love will be fourfold.'

'If – if,' said Nicholas, and although he smiled, it was a melancholy smile. 'Not only ourselves, but the whole future history of England can rest on that inconsiderable word. There is no certainty that the Queen will bear a son, or that he will live if she does. The King has been singularly unfortunate in his two previous wives.'

'But that, surely, was because they were not real marriages,' Annis said eagerly. 'Queen Katherine was first the wife of the King's brother, and the second union was unhallowed. As for Anne Boleyn, she was a witch and fearfully wicked.'

They were walking through the yew garden, on so cold and dreary a morning that nobody from the palace was abroad. None the less Nicholas glanced round him before he said in a low, cautious voice: 'It is dangerous to mention the late Queen's name, or at least to mention it with compassion; but I for one do not subscribe to all the stories that are whispered about her. She had much to endure, poor courageous lady, and had she been a witch would she not have been able to save herself from her terrible fate?'

'Perhaps the power went out of her; but if she really had five fingers on one hand she must have been a witch, for that is one of the signs,' Annis replied positively.

'Which is superstition as foolish as that which makes our present Queen believe that when she is near you, your strength flows into her. My uncle had much regard for Queen Anne, and she was sorely beset and unhappy. Queen Jane may not have been responsible, but . . .'

'She vows that she was not, Nicholas. Oh, not to me, but to Anne Boleyn herself, or the shade which hovers near her. She speaks to it sometimes, pleads with it in mortal fear, protesting that she would have saved her if she could. It is the fever of the blood which comes and goes in her, but sometimes such is the persuasion of her fantasy that I have almost seemed to see a figure beside her.'

'A fantasy indeed,' said Nicholas firmly. 'Queen Anne's sufferings purged her sins. Her penitential sojourn in Purgatory must have been brief, and now she is in Heaven. That was her own belief, clearly stated on the scaffold. She went to her death with joy, having cast off the desire to live. What fiendish punishing it would be to return her to this earth, in order to torment her supplanter for whom her spirit can feel nought but compassion. Can even the Queen suppose that Anne now envies her?'

'Perhaps she does. People who are alive, who are loved as the Queen is loved, and who have so much future hope, do not imagine that it is better to be dead. I dread the thought of it, Nicholas. I shall always love life . . . the growing things . . . trees, flowers, even the feel of the good earth; the wind that stirs my hair and the rain and the sun. I want to live to be old, very old; to have my children and my grandchildren around me. Is not that a natural wish?'

'Indeed it is, especially for Demeter.' But although Nicholas smiled down into her face, his eyes were sad.

'Natural for you, too. Oh, my love, have faith. Pray that we may be together on earth as husband and wife, and for many years before we love again in heaven.'

There was a passion and entreaty in Annis's voice to which Nicholas responded. Her hood had fallen back from her hair, and he stroked it gently as he drew her to him, and then kissed her.

'Most certainly I will pray for it,' he said, 'and if our marriage can be contrived by the King's grace, no man will be happier than I. Mayhap I cling less strongly to life than you, for its miseries sometimes seem to me to be greater than its joys; but such as there are would be found in your arms, that I doubt not.'

Annis would not allow herself to feel defeated by the melancholy and resignation which she sensed were a part of his nature. She was sure that she loved life enough for the two of them and had resolution enough too.

Perhaps it was true that she had a closer kinship with the fertile earth than most people, for the very feel of it beneath her feet was strongly sweet. Of herbs, both beneficial and poisonous which grew in the fields and hedgerows, there was little that she did not know; it was the power of the earth that it could give both life and death.

35

That primitive loving had been so natural to Annis that she had scarcely considered it, but in her intelligent though immature mind she was now conscious of a growing power, though it would probably have lain latent had it not been for the Queen, who from her first glance at her had believed she transmitted strength and life. Even that she had dismissed as a fantasy, until having met Nicholas she was impressed by his half-playful insistence that she was akin to Ceres, the Earth Mother.

Later that day, Susan Partridge came upon her gazing at herself in a mirror which hung upon a wall of her bedchamber. It was a faulty mirror, but even so there was an unusual brilliance of colour in the image it reflected. Annis's features were not remarkable. Her nose was near to a snub, her eyes were not the enormous, heavy-lidded eyes considered essential to beauty, her upper lip was a shade too long, and her mouth was wide; but her fair hair sprang back from her wide brow in a profusion of waves and curls; her eyes were brightly blue and her creamy skin, with an overlay of tan, suggested the blush on a ripe peach. Her lips were carmine, her teeth as white as peeled almonds and of much the same shape; her neck was a firm column, and her tall body with its full bosom and long, strong legs, could only be faulted because a slender grace, narrow feet and delicate, useless hands were generally admired.

Annis, too, had admired a type of beauty opposite to her own, but now her ideas were veering. Such a contented smile broke over her face that Susan laughed at her. Although only three weeks older than Annis, she had worked at Pleasance from childhood and had never been innocently carefree.

'My lady stepmother may be as jealous of my looks as she was of my father's love for me,' said Annis, turning from the mirror.

'Father Benedict at home preaches from the pulpit that beauty is a snare, and that vanity is a sin,' Susan reproved, though indulgently.

'If you were given three wishes, would not your first be to ask for beauty?' Annis retorted.

Susan, who even without the pock-marks which disfigured her face could never have been anything but plain, shook her head : 'I have seen too many brought to grief by it,' she said. "'Tis better for a woman to be deft at weaving and to have a light hand with pastry, for such will last throughout life. With age, eyes lose their sparkle and the skin coarsens and fades. Come Michaelmas next year, Tam Reynolds, the herdsman and I, will be wed. He says my venison pasties are such as to ravish any man's heart, and I have saved a third of my wages for these last five years. I have a full stocking to help us on our way.'

Annis was at once interested. 'I did not know you planned to wed. Doubtless all you say is true, and I will ask my father to add some angels to your stocking.'

Susan thanked her, though she was not greatly impressed by this grand manner. It was well known that it was Lady Grenton, not his daughter, who influenced Sir Lucian, and her ladyship was a skin-flint who kept a sharp eye on every groat as well as every pound of butter and pint of cream produced in the dairy. Still, it was true that she had a sense of what was right and fitting, and Susan's young mistress had had her purse filled with angels when she left home.

As though it suddenly occurred to Annis that she might be unable to keep her promise, she said : 'When we leave here, I will give you all that is left in my purse. It would be foolish to return with money, for it would be taken from me by her ladyship. But you must bear me out when I tell her of causes of expenditure which I could not avoid.'

It was easy to obtain such a promise from the gratified Susan who was now gazing at her with surprise, realizing how greatly she had changed in a few weeks. Annis, too, was conscious of change, though what girl, she thought, would not alter with a lover such as Nicholas? Now, mindful of the difficulties before her and of her lack of power, it had struck her that it would be as well to enlist the loyalty of the humble Susan. She might be of use. Who could tell?

In the days that followed, Annis had need of all her confidence, for a voluminous letter arrived by messenger from Lady Grenton. As Annis skimmed through the first sheet, she was struck by her stepmother's cordiality. Sir Lucian, she wrote, was in better health. He had been well enough to walk in the garden, and his gout had eased. Lady Grenton had taken advantage of it to entertain a few guests, and that had put Sir Lucian in great spirits. There was much talk in the district about the command which had taken Annis to Hampton and about the favour that the Queen had shown her, with the result that at last Lady Grenton was happy to tell her that an offer had been made for her hand.

At that point, it was necessary to turn the page, as Lady Grenton had used up all the space on the first one. Annis, with her eyes dilated, read on, her heart beating rapidly.

Sir Hugh Derevale, Lady Grenton wrote, had one day come over on horseback from his estate at Swordel, and he had been closeted with Annis's father for a full hour. Negotiations for a betrothal contract were now in process, and it was to be hoped that these would go through smoothly. Lady Grenton was sure that Annis would be deeply gratified. Sir Hugh was a fine and sober gentleman of good repute, *and both your father and I, my dear daughter,* so Lady Grenton stated, *will be happy to entrust you to his care.*

With a gasp of rage, Annis stared at the written words. Her father must be mad; her stepmother was an evil witch to imagine that she would consent to marry such as Sir Hugh Derevale. She would have refused, even had she not met and loved Nicholas, for Sir Hugh was sixty if he was a day. He had been a widower for several years and had five daughters, all married, who had children of their own. Moreover, though he was a baronet, he was by no means rich, and lived in a shabby house on a neglected estate. He was said to have impoverished himself in order to marry off his daughters with generous dowries. A wondrous kind and unselfish father, so said his neighbours.

Well, and so he might be, fumed Annis, pacing her room with her stepmother's letter crumpled in her hand, but it must be the goodly amount of *her* rumoured dowry which had induced him to offer for her, and it was monstrous to consider marrying off a girl of eighteen to a man old enough to be her grandfather.

She had met him, all told, less than a score of times, though he had occasionally visited Pleasance during her mother's lifetime. As a small child he had dandled her on his knee, and even then she had been repelled by his red face, loud laugh and stringy red hair. She remembered with nausea that there had been tufts of the same reddish hair sprouting from his ears and nostrils.

'I would rather die,' vowed Annis, 'and if by some insanity I allowed myself to be forced into marriage with him, why then it would be he who would soon die. There are ways. I would find a way.'

Other wives – other poor girls so beset – must also have found ways by which they could rid themselves of a spouse they loathed. Only this present week Susan, who revelled in gruesome stories, had told her of a farmer's wife whose much older husband had been a brute when he was in drink and thrashed her unmercifully. The young wife's parents had sold her to him because they were heavily in his debt, and they had been helpless to succour her, or so it was thought, only, and here Susan had spoken in a whisper, the girl's mother was said to have become quite desperate at her daughter's plight, and it was rumoured that she had brought about his death.

In her cottage garden there were toads and she had been seen collecting them, and then she had taken a cask of home-brewed ale over to her son-in-law and he had fallen sick and after a while he died. Much was suspected but there was no proof, and the man's intemperate habits, and the fact that he had fallen down in a fit one winter evening and had lain out until morning in the rain and sleet, was said by the apothecary to have brought about his death. But the whispering villagers thought differently, though nobody publicly accused, and if it came to that, said Susan, nobody blamed the girl's mother.

The story horrified Annis, for she knew the family of whom this story was told. She recalled the young widow who had been thin and pale, almost withered-looking, and knowing nothing of the circumstances Annis had then thought she must be pining for the husband she had lost. The mother was a sturdy woman, still only in early middle-age, with a mild, round, kindly face, and a benevolent smile. Occasionally in the spring, when there was the great annual scouring and polishing and cleansing, she had been employed at Pleasance as a wash-woman.

Annis shuddered. The story might have no foundation, and

yet . . . it was known that toads were poisonous. You took one, the biggest you could find, and then . . . well, if you pricked it several times and put it in a closed vessel, and then when it was dead took the poisonous juice which it had shed as an animal might shed blood, and mixed it with any drink or sauce; who would know, since the liquor itself was tasteless? You might not succeed at first, but with patience and persistence you would in the end achieve the desired result.

Annis tore Lady Grenton's letter into fragments. She would never consent. Nobody could force her. To do that, she would have to be dragged unconscious to the church, and if that were possible, who then would utter her vows? They would never, swore Annis, pass her lips.

✳ CHAPTER 6 ✳

There was little opportunity for Annis to brood or to lash herself into wrath over Lady Grenton's letter, for on the next day the Queen started in labour.

Throughout the first stage Annis was present. The Queen sent for her, insisting that she was of more benefit to her than any physician or midwife; and indeed while the pains were slight and the Queen cheerful, it did seem, and not for the first time, that she derived consolation from Annis's attendance. It was not only that she was strong and glowing, but that she was ignorant and did not share the apprehension of the midwives or the grave-faced apothecaries; all of whom anticipated a hard birth, if only because of the Queen's abnormally narrow hips and her weakness throughout pregnancy.

Later, it was difficult. Annis was shocked to witness the Queen's suffering. Then, trembling, useless and ignored, she crouched by the bed, listening with horror to sobs and groans; appalled by the sight of the ravaged face and writhing body.

None of the customary treatments appeared to afford the Queen any relief. She gazed with distraught eyes at those who clustered round her, and they for their part exchanged bewildered and panic-stricken glances as delirious words tumbled from her parched lips. It was only too evident that she saw that which was invisible to them, and cried out to it for mercy.

'I call upon the King's grace to witness that I had no hand in it,' the Queen raved. 'Have I not told you so before, again and again? Oh Harry, Harry, why are you not here to convince her?'

At last, in desperation, a message was sent to the King. He, since the start of the Queen's travail, had made repeated enquiries as to her state, and it was no longer possible to assure him that all was going well, since she was not only labouring to bring her child into the world but was also in contact with some dark shade whom, so she believed, was gloating over her agony.

Annis was ordered from the room, but she was still crouching against the wall when the King entered. Harshly he issued commands. For a short while he must be left alone with the Queen. He, better than a priest, could exorcise an imagined demon, and could convince her that by the power of his divine Kinghood he had banished it.

Tender and pitying as he lifted his tortured wife in his arms and bent over her, Annis for a fleeting second saw him at his best. Then she was thrust into the passage, and the other attendants soon joined her. From within they could all hear the murmur of the King's voice, and presently the Queen's cries were stilled. There was a long interval before the door opened, and the King emerged, his face glistening with sweat.

He threw a few curt words to those who waited. The Queen was consoled; her pains had abated and she was drowsing. He strode away but for an instant his gaze fell upon Annis's crouching form and the royal hand lightly touched her shoulder. With a bleak smile he remarked that the Queen had no further immediate need of her Talisman, and that she might go to her room and rest.

Annis was only too thankful to obey. For the first time she realized something of the King's magnetism. She had often wondered if the young Queen had any real love for him, but now it seemed possible that she had. In her extremity she had called for him and he had not failed her. If Anne Boleyn's vengeful spirit had indeed been present, he had routed it.

The long hours dragged away. Excitement and speculation were swamped by a weary boredom. The King kept to his own suite, and with the absence of music and singing the silence was profound.

Not until the following day, a Friday, the 12th of October, did the Queen give birth to the long-desired heir. By then she was completely exhausted, and it was some hours before she realized that the King at last had his heart's desire. Henry could not do enough to express his gratitude and triumphant joy. There were costly jewels with which to deck the Queen and the baby boy, and gifts and lesser jewels for all those who had rendered the least service through the crucial hours. Annis became the recipient of a ruby and diamond brooch formed in the initials H and J. It was the replica of others given to the Queen's ladies, and had been designed weeks ago in preparation for the great event.

Another day and night passed, and then Annis was summoned to the Queen's bedside.

Although rejoicing was prevalent, not only at Hampton Court, so Annis heard it said, but throughout the kingdom, this seemed strangely inappropriate when she first saw the Queen who looked even more ill than when she had writhed in agony. Now her face was hollow-cheeked and the colour of parchment; her eyes were sunken and her lips colourless. She could speak but feebly, though she smiled at Annis and told her she was wonderfully happy. She was in no pain, and would soon be stronger. The infant Prince was a fine hearty boy, and the King was surpassingly proud of him. Annis was to stay beside her as she had done in the weeks before her trial, but first she must see the little Prince.

Annis gazed with curiosity at the tiny, crumpled face. The baby was decked out in silk and satin, with a great diamond sparkling in his embroidered cap. How strange it was that this midget who whimpered as she bent over him was the future King of England.

Meanwhile, thanksgiving services were held at St Paul's and the city churches; bonfires were alight in the London streets, and there was a constant volleying of guns. Free feasts were ordered for the poor; messengers were sent throughout the realm to spread the glad news.

At Hampton Court Palace an enormous banquet was held, and Annis was allowed to attend it. Her place was at one of the least important tables, but little she cared for Nicholas was sitting opposite to her. Afterwards they danced together in the great hall.

Now Annis had the opportunity to consider her future. She hesitated, wondering whether or not to tell Nicholas of her stepmother's letter, but she finally decided against it. At the best of times he was not a hopeful person, and this news might upset him, even more than it had upset her. As it was, he was inclined to think there was some promise for them. It was a time of universal delight; the King could scarcely contain himself for joy, and it did seem possible that as the Queen had shown Annis such favour, she might be prevailed upon to interest herself in their future.

On the Monday at midnight the royal baby was baptized in the palace chapel, and Annis with several of the Queen's ladies was amongst the spectators. Had it not been for the odious thought of Sir Hugh Derevale, she would have dwelt with pleasure on the description she could give of the wonderful event on her return to Pleasance.

A myriad tapers illuminated the scene and shone down on the silver font. When the procession formed, all smiled to see the little Lady Elizabeth in gorgeous clothes, bearing the chrism and herself carried by Lord Beauchamp. The Lady Mary too had discarded her usual, dark, rich gown, and was in a gold and silver dress. The baby Prince was borne in upon a litter beneath a canopy.

At the conclusion of the ceremony the Lady Elizabeth walked instead of being carried. The Lady Mary held her hand and a lady of the Court carried her train.

During the christening the King stayed beside the Queen's bed. He had never loved her better, and the apothecaries assured him she was making a rapid recovery; gathering strength with every hour that passed.

Nobody doubted it. Her attendants had wrapped her in a cloak embroidered with gold and pearls; her crown was placed on her head, and when the trumpets sounded she was lifted from her bed to sit in a great chair and receive the Prince in her arms. Looking down upon the baby she tried to speak and could not. She would have found it impossible to hold him but that the King supported the little form.

The royal father smiled with amusement and joy when the baby yawned widely. He called the Queen's attention to his rosy cheeks and the fair hair which had escaped from the band of the jewelled hat, but the Queen who seemed half-dead with fatigue could conjure up no answering smile.

✳ CHAPTER 7 ✳

Annis contracted a heavy cold and was forced to stay in her own room. She never knew if during those days the Queen wanted her or asked for her, but she did hear that her royal mistress had fallen into an illness which puzzled all her physicians. She had seemed to be recovering from the effects of childbirth; but now she was very weak and becoming weaker.

Annis, hoarse, sneezing and feverish, was too sorry for herself to give much thought to the Queen, and by the time she was better all was over.

A weeping lady-in-waiting told her that the Queen had been beyond speech for the last three days before her death. She had fallen into a stupor from which nobody could arouse her, not even the King.

Annis's hopes of royal support in her love affair vanished with the Queen's death. She had become of no account. The King, said to be inconsolable, kept to his own apartments. Every courtier and lady, everyone employed at the palace down to the most humble scullion was garbed by the King's command in deepest black. Mourning garments were fashioned with haste by a bevy of clothiers who were accommodated at the palace. Annis was issued with black gowns and cloaks, such as those in which the maids of honour were now shrouded. Susan had the coarser garments allotted to the palace menials. All were forbidden to leave the precincts during the two weeks in which the dead Queen lay in state.

Her ladies knelt around the bier upon which lay the still form covered with a pall of cloth of gold. Candles burned there night and day, and the Lady Mary, as chief mourner, spent hours on her knees, her vigil broken only by brief hours for sleep and food. But although nobody was allowed to leave the palace, many messengers from home and abroad arrived there, some from foreign royal courts bearing messages of sympathy. Amongst these were two servants who had been sent from Pleasance with a letter for Annis.

Lady Grenton, after a few words of formal lament for the Queen, informed her stepdaughter that Sir Lucian, after weeks of improved health, had been taken by a sudden apoplexy which was the cause of great concern. She instructed Annis to apply for permission to leave the palace and to return to Pleasance forthwith. Distractedly, Annis in her ignorance wondered to whom she could apply, and when she confided in one of the elderly ladies-in-waiting who had shown some slight interest in her, the other suggested that she might seek the advice of the Lady Mary, taking advantage of one of the brief intervals when she was forced to abandon the death vigil.

With trepidation Annis did so, falling on her knees in the path of the King's daughter as she walked slowly along the corridor to her own suite of rooms. Mary, scarcely recognizable in her habiliments of woe, put back the black veil from her face to gaze down at the kneeling Annis, and in silence heard her plea. Mary's face was deadly pale, her eyes swollen with much weeping and little sleep, but she was kind and concerned.

After consideration, she said she would take the responsibility of allowing Annis to leave. She would give instructions and inform the Comptroller, who in view of the King's expressed commands might be uncertain how to act. It was unlikely that His Majesty would hear of her departure, or give

45

a thought to the country girl whom the Queen in her fantasy had believed to be her Talisman; but if he did, the Lady Mary would explain matters to him. She could have said, though she did not, that at this time she was the being nearest to the King. He would see her when he would see nobody else.

For Annis there was a final meeting with Nicholas in the library, where during these mournful days he had been able to seclude himself, as much forgotten as she was. They parted with tears, and on his side with little hope that they could ever come together again, for Annis lacked the hardihood to point out that if her father died, it might well be possible for them to marry. Nicholas, who had a lover's natural illusions, would have been shocked had he realized that she was already looking beyond to when Sir Lucian would be gone, and she his heiress and owner of Pleasance. He had persuaded himself that she was stunned by grief at her father's illness.

Grieved she was, but not stunned. Youth and life were Annis's preoccupations, more especially life. Death was the enemy, but when it had conquered it was useless to brood over it. The long death vigil for the Queen seemed senseless to Annis, and all her hedonism revolted against it. She was thankful to be spared the protracted ordeal of the funeral, though had she wished she could have followed as one of the cortège with the rest of the late Queen's attendants. Jane was to be buried at Windsor, and with great pageantry. But pageantry, thought Annis, was incongruous when it was associated with death whose triumph should be minimized.

As for her father, though she loved him, some instinct told her that he was already dead, and her moods veered, sometimes heavy with sadness but sometimes lifted with a new sense of importance.

The November weather was so inclement that on the homeward way two nights instead of one were spent at wayside inns, where much the same discomfort was suffered as on the journey to Hampton.

To Susan, with whom Annis had become on more familiar terms, for all at the palace being strangers there they had clung together, she could speak freely, and that she did when they were alone. Susan already knew of the attachment to Nicholas Colton and was sympathetic. She had seen Nicholas once or twice and considered him a goodly gentleman, certainly a far more suitable match for her than the elderly Sir Hugh Derevale.

Now, believing as Annis believed, that she was already the mistress of Pleasance, Susan showed her a far greater respect, and Annis took pleasure in assuring her that if this was the case, she would do well by Susan. She would give her a marriage portion and a cottage on the estate which she would have furnished for her.

Susan could scarcely believe her ears. She was afraid to take Annis seriously. She could expect nothing from Sir Lucian if he lived, for Lady Grenton who found her satisfactory would be annoyed at her leaving, and would do nothing for her. She said so.

'I shall miss you too, and be sorry to lose you,' said Annis, 'but I would like you to be happy. I know now what it means to be in love, and you are, aren't you?'

Susan, red in the face and looking plainer than ever, assured Annis that she was. Her Tam was a handsome fellow, she said, and a year younger than herself. Several of the village girls had set their caps at him, and sometimes this had caused quarrels, for Tam, Susan admitted, though he was so sensible and thought much of her cooking and steadiness and being ready to save, was none the less tempted by a pretty face. That would not worry Susan once they were married, for she'd make a comfortable home for him and between them they would prosper. It was the months of being secretly tokened to him which irked her.

Annis might dread to hear of her father's death, even though it would give her Nicholas, but Susan had no such divided mind. She now hoped eagerly that such was the case. It would be a grand thing to see the hard and miserly Lady Grenton forced to step down for the young mistress, and there would be no need to wait until next Michaelmas if she was to be given a furnished cottage and a marriage portion.

When on the third day of their journey they were jolted

47

down the avenue by weary, mud-splashed horses, driven by a coachman who had been in mortal terror through reports that highwaymen had recently robbed several coaches and were still at large, Susan's eyes flickered with joy on seeing that every blind was closely drawn across the windows.

Annis immediately burst into tears and had to be comforted. It was a melancholy thing to be told that Sir Lucian had recovered consciousness before the end and had asked for her. He had smiled when told that she was on her homeward way, but had died less than an hour later.

Even Lady Grenton seemed moved by Annis's grief. She embraced Annis and once again addressed her as daughter. Calm and dignified, and far from incapable through distress, Lady Grenton had already made most of the arrangements for her husband's burial.

Decency demanded that no immediate business should be discussed. The few neighbours with whom Isabel retained a friendship rallied to support one who appeared to need no support, and it was generally conceded that she showed great courage and resignation.

Annis had the curious conviction that her stepmother, for all her show of dignified sorrow, was yet immersed in some secret satisfaction. It would have been improper during those first days of mourning for a widow to occupy herself more than was absolutely necessary with household tasks, and she who had never been idle but had in leisure hours worked at tapestry or embroidery, now seemed oddly different as she sat with her hands folded on her black skirts.

It was not until after the funeral that mention was made of Sir Hugh Derevale, though he with several of Sir Lucian's acquaintances as well as many of the villagers and servants were in the church and had stood around the grave.

When the last mourner departed after the plenteous but sombre funeral feast at Pleasance, the two women sat together in the sitting-room they commonly used, which was warmer and more comfortable at this time of year than the great drawing-room, and then Lady Grenton said: 'You must have much to tell me of your stay at Court, though this has not been the time to question you about it. Poor child,

48

you have passed through a heavy trial with the death of the Queen's grace, and now our own great loss. The favour that was shown to you made an impression here, and as I told you when I wrote to you, there is now a good hope for your future, which should help to cheer you.'

Annis braced herself for wordy combat: 'How should it cheer me, madam?'

'Sir Hugh Derevale is a good, kind, honourable man of excellent lineage. He will make you a worthy husband, and although he is not rich, your dowry will be substantial and will no doubt be put to good use. Sir Hugh's daughters have been given their portions, and will be no further charge upon him. For the last few years I have been training you in housewifely lore, and you should now be competent to manage your own establishment. There is no reason why your marriage should not be as successful as my own. I, too, married one who was considerably my senior, and my fortune was used for the benefit of Pleasance. There is a resemblance between my case and the future planned for you.'

'I can see very little resemblance,' said Annis. 'You were ten years older than I am now when you married my father who was much younger than Sir Hugh. Besides, you loved him. He was a fine, handsome man. Sir Hugh is old enough to be my grandfather, he is not at all handsome; to me he is horrible. I will never marry him. Why should I? Especially now, when my father is dead, and I am mistress here.'

'Mistress here? What fancy is this?' Lady Grenton enquired with raised brows.

'It is my home. As my father had no sons, it became mine on his death. I have always known that that was how it would be.'

Gazing at her steadily, Lady Grenton shook her head. 'You have been misinformed.'

Annis felt as though her heart was beating in her throat. She said thickly: 'How can that be? I know the history of Pleasance. Ever since it was built long ago when Edward IV was king, it has descended from father to son, or if there was no son, to the eldest daughter, who when she married required her husband to take the name of Grenton. That

49

has happened twice. The last female owner of Pleasance was my great-grandmother. There has been no break in the line since the building of Pleasance, though the title was not conferred until my grandfather's day. Now the title is extinct since my father had no male relations, but Pleasance is mine. Your ladyship saw fit to sell the property that your parents left you, for you knew that if my father died first there was the Dower House here to which you would retire; though doubtless it would suit you well if I married Sir Hugh and lived at Derevale Manor, leaving you in charge of Pleasance.'

'I see,' said Lady Grenton, 'that you have industriously studied the family history. It does so happen that the ownership of Pleasance has been in no dispute, and it is not in dispute now, for when I married your father, certain provisions were made. Just provisions as my fortune was used to repair the estate and to make it possible for your father and you to continue to live here. It was recognized that he would probably die before me and this being so, a Deed was drawn up which in the event of there being no son to succeed, ensures me a life tenancy of Pleasance. I regret if it is a shock to you, Annis, though had you given more thought to the matter, you would have surely realized that your father, having taken all I had, could not in justice leave me without maintenance.'

For a full minute Annis had nothing to say. She was stunned and her face slowly paled. Lady Grenton said with false gentleness : 'I have been appointed your guardian, and I cannot of course turn you away from Pleasance, nor would I wish to, though as we are unsympathetic to each other you will be better placed in an establishment of your own. But it would be more peaceable to discuss this further with Preston, the attorney, who will be calling here tomorrow with papers that it is necessary for me to sign, and he will explain all to you.'

Annis found her voice : 'If what you say is true, it is clear enough. You have a claim to live here unless you marry again. But even so, you can never feel you are the real mistress of Pleasance which will be mine eventually.'

'That is not certain.' Lady Grenton transferred her gaze from her stepdaughter's face to the fire, smiling with her eyes fixed on the glowing embers as though a pleasing picture had formed there.

'What do you mean?' The question was put with dread. It was plain to Annis that her stepmother was holding in reserve some secret knowledge which was a source of triumph and joy. Afterwards, she wondered at her dullness because no suspicion of the truth struck her.

'There may yet be an heir,' said Lady Grenton. 'I am *enceinte*. Your father knew this not long before his death and it gave him great happiness. I was not certain of it when you left for Hampton, otherwise I might have told you . . . I was afraid to be too hopeful; but while you were away I consulted Dr Burnett, and now there is no doubt.'

'I – I . . .' Annis could not speak. Her eyes were burning; she tasted salt in her mouth. She clenched her hands in speechless rage.

Lady Grenton rose. Moving towards the door, she stopped by Annis's chair, and put her hand on the girl's shoulder. 'No doubt it is a shock to you,' she said, 'though surely you must have known it was a possibility. 'Tis a sad thing that although I have endeavoured to win your affection, I have so signally failed. If I had not, you might have rejoiced with me in the alleviation of my widow's sorrow.'

'The baby may be another girl.'

'That is a possibility,' Lady Grenton admitted.

But her conviction that she would bear a son was evident to Annis. Not that this was of great significance. Such conviction was no more than the force of her own wish. Had not Anne Boleyn been certain when she was carrying her girl child that she was about to give a future king to England?

'When you have had time for thought,' said Lady Grenton, 'you will, being not without sense, realize that as Lady Derevale and the mistress of Derevale Manor you will be in a far happier situation.'

Annis lay sobbing on her bed. She had shut herself into her room, had drawn the bolt on the door, and had been alone there for hours. Nobody had disturbed her. Lady Grenton having said all that she desired to say was well content.

It was not until late in the evening that there was a tap on the door. At first Annis was stubbornly silent, resolved not to answer, but then she heard Susan's voice.

'Let me in, please, Mistress,' Susan pleaded. 'I have brought you some broth and another candle. Yours must be almost spent for the hours it has been burning.'

Not averse now to receive comfort, Annis got off the bed and unbolted the door. Susan, exclaiming with concern at her tear-disfigured face, set down a tray upon which there was in addition to the cup of soup, a manchet of freshly baked bread and a small cheese. She coaxed Annis to eat as she might have coaxed a child.

'Her ladyship might well have pity for you and not only for herself,' Susan grumbled. 'A daughter has as much cause for grief as a wife.'

Annis having discovered she was hungry had eaten all that was on the tray. Now she said miserably : 'It is not only that. Oh Susan, I shall be unable to keep my promise about the cottage and furnishing it for you. I doubt if I shall have a penny, unless I marry Sir Hugh, or if not he, some other horrible man of her ladyship's choosing. I shall even be grudged a home here, and as for the one I do love . . .'

More tears flowed as she considered the hopeless outlook. If it were true that her father had legally arranged for Lady Grenton to be her guardian, she would have to obey her, and she would never be allowed to marry Nicholas who had not the means to support a wife. Susan stared at her in blank dismay, and then, forgetful that it was an impertinence, she started to question her.

Annis was in no state of mind to give a thought to a servant's undue familiarity, though for the last four years Lady Grenton had impressed upon her that she was far too friendly with menials. This, to one who for two neglected years had depended on them, had seemed an absurdity.

Within a few minutes, Susan heard that for so long as Lady Grenton lived, Pleasance was hers. The fact that she was bearing a child, who should it be a male would automatically disinherit Annis, hardly made matters worse. Susan, believing her young mistress to be in possession, had been gloating over her own prospects and had told her sweetheart about them.

'She's strong and healthy,' said Susan bitterly. 'She's not so much older than me. She could live to be ninety.'

'I've never known anyone to live as long as that,' Annis objected.

'Then seventy or eighty. There are ancients of that age, even in this village. By the time her ladyship's that old, little good Pleasance 'ull be to you, if you're still living.'

'I know, I know, Susan. I've been lying here for hours thinking of it. Oh, what's to become of me? I'd rather die than marry that horrible man . . . when I think of being bedded with him – I couldn't, Susan.'

'No more you shall,' said Susan, roughly comforting.

Eighteen though she was, Annis childishly nestled to her, digging her chin into Susan's bosom, grateful for the clasp of her arms. There was something earthily reassuring about the mingled soap and sweat which was Susan's familiar aroma.

'But it's my only chance of getting away from her,' Annis moaned. 'It's just as you say, she's strong and healthy and will live to be very old.'

'I said as how she *could* live to be that age; but there's no surety. Your own poor mother was carried off sudden. I remember it clear enough. There's a many who die in childbed or before it. Not only Queens, but ordinary people.'

'She won't. She isn't delicate as the Queen was.'

'It isn't always those who seem the strongest who turn out to be. There's sickness and weakness that comes on many women when they're in her way, and she's pining too for the loss of her man.'

'I don't believe she *is* pining, Susan. She loved my father when she married him I dare say, but he's been a care on her for a long time, and now she's set her heart on the baby and on triumphing over me, if it's a boy. That's a satisfaction to her.'

'Maybe it won't be for long.'

Susan unwound Annis's arms and moved away from her. She sat down in a high-backed, rush-seated chair at the foot of the bed. There were two candles alight now; the one that had burnt low, and the other a thick, tall one that Susan, unpermitted, must have taken from the store-room. It gave a steady light, but the flickering of the expiring candle threw odd shadows on Susan's rough-hewn face, giving it an unfamiliar look. At first Annis could not put a name to that look and then the word power occurred to her, though that seemed absurd, for what was Susan after all except an ignorant servant-girl who all her life had obeyed orders?

'Did you mean it, Mistress, when you said you'd do that as would set me and Tam up for life?' she asked abruptly.

'You know I meant it, though a cottage and furniture and a marriage present wouldn't do as much as that for you.'

'A present,' said Susan slowly, 'can be big or small. If you was in her ladyship's shoes, maybe you'd make it a worthwhile present.'

'Oh yes, I would,' and Annis sighed heavily.

'Then what would you say to putting it down in writing, clear to be read?'

Annis, who had been huddled in the bedclothes, sat upright in her astonishment. 'But what would be the good of that, Susan? It's not likely I'll ever have Pleasance . . . never if she has a son, and not for years anyway.'

Susan considered her in silence, hesitated, bit on a workworn thumb, and then said: 'You write that down for me, deary, and we'll see about it. There used to be paper and a quill and ink in the desk yonder.'

With Annis's wondering eyes fixed on her, Susan found writing materials, spread them on the desk that had once been in the schoolroom, and placed a chair before it.

'Why do you want me to write?' Annis said irritably. 'You can't read – or I suppose you can't.'

'I can, if it's writ plain,' retorted Susan. 'When you was no more than a babby I was going to the village school the master set up. A great one he was in those days, and all for learning us folks to read and write and add figures. I've forgot a lot of it, but I still remember enough as will do me. Now sit you down and write that when you are mistress of Pleasance, you'll set up your faithful servant Susan Partridge in a fine, new cottage with all its furnishings, and fifty gold pieces a year for as long as she lives.'

Sitting at the desk, with the pen in her hand, Annis looked at Susan with startled eyes. 'But that's a great deal of money, or if it went on for long, it could be.'

'I trow you won't think it too much for all that'll be yourn,' Susan answered. 'You do as I say, and hold your peace and mayhap her grand ladyship won't trouble you for long.'

'I don't understand you.' Annis spoke on an uncertain note of fear.

'And don't need to, deary. The less you know the better. Just write as I've said, and then I'll have the promise in my keeping.'

'Susan . . . I . . .' The faltering voice broke off. Annis with her heart thudding, murmured : 'You frighten me.'

The other laughed : 'You frightened of Susan, who's known you from when you was so little you couldn't stand steady on your feet — that you're not! Just you write on the paper, and then we'll say no more about it. I'll tuck you up snug in bed and you'll sleep and forget it all. It's my business then. You've done your part.'

'Are you — do you know a witch — someone who can . . .?'

'Can what?'

'Can bring such things to pass? I've heard that there are such — perhaps even living near here.'

Susan laughed again, but this time scornfully : 'There's none that I know on, or if there is, I'm as good with my spells as any of them. Now, don't go to start away from me, Mistress, for it's nought but a joke. What would such as I know of spells and witches?'

'But you're speaking so oddly,' said Annis feebly.

'Maybe that's through the disappointment I've took this

55

day. You have, too – but it's as bad for me. Write down your promise now. 'Twon't cost you nought if luck favours her ladyship.'

Annis, after a brief pause, bent over the sheet spread before her. She wrote swiftly in large letters, and with a flourish signed her name. She handed the paper to Susan, who standing between the candles, the steady and the flickering light, laboriously read the few lines. Her lips curled in a contented smile.

Annis said fretfully: 'It's nothing but foolishness.'

'Maybe it is, maybe it's not. Haven't I said to forget it?'

Although it was long since Susan or any of the servants had ordered her about as they had when she was a child, Annis was so startled and over-awed that she did not resent it.

Rolling the paper, Susan thrust it down the neck of her bodice and then turned to the bed and smoothed the tossed rugs and blankets. With competent hands she helped Annis to undress and tucked her snugly beneath the coverings. She bade her good night with the familiarity of a nurse to her charge, snuffed out the good candle with a pinch of her fingers and went from the room.

The opening and closing of the door finally quenched the candle that was already spent. In the darkness Annis lay and shivered as though with cold, though deep within her there was a warmth of reassurance which she dared not analyse.

PART TWO
1584-1594

Lucilla Grenton first saw Pleasance when she was ten years old, and the impact it made upon her young mind was never throughout her life to be forgotten. In her hearing, her father had often spoken of his boyhood home, referring to it as the old house or the old place; not apparently having any particular wish to see it again, or regretting the haphazard life to which his calling as an actor committed his wife and children.

Not that Robert or Lucilla had any idea that by more conventional standards their lives were unsettled. Their early childhood was happy for their father and mother were tender parents, though even after ten years of marriage they were so ardently in love that the twins born to Joan Grenton were not the objects of an intense devotion.

Whereas many wives of popular players who toured the country when they were not performing at the London theatres, either lived with their families or set up permanent homes in London, to which their husbands returned as often as they might, Joan refused to be parted from her Jeremy, and with her two children accompanied him on his travels.

The twins, therefore, became accustomed to the indifferent comfort of lodgings, and accepted them as a matter of course. Schooling was intermittent until they were between seven and eight years old. Then, Jeremy Grenton having joined James Burbage, whose players were under the patronage of the great Earl of Leicester, finally rented a house in Shoreditch, conveniently near to the building known as The Theatre which had only recently been erected. Almost within hailing distance was The Curtain, a rival theatre which was built within a few months of the first building.

A coterie of players swiftly grew up around the two theatres and lived practically in a world of their own, only touring if there were fierce outbreaks of the plague in London when, by law, all theatres were closed and the members of the companies became strolling players until the epidemic abated.

The Grenton twins mixed freely with the children of other players, and attended a Shoreditch school which had been started in the district by an enterprising master. Joan Grenton was thrifty and saving, her children were well-clad and fed and the atmosphere of their home was singularly harmonious.

Jeremy Grenton was a sweet-tempered man who in his spare time was ready to frolic with the twins, to tell them stories both real and fanciful, and when from time to time they sat amongst the audience on either side of their mother and watched their handsome father in heroic roles on the stage. They admired him profoundly. From Jeremy they heard vivid descriptions of the occasion when the company was commanded to Greenwich Palace to appear before the great Queen herself, and then were told of the extraordinary incident of the brooch which was Jeremy's most treasured possession.

It had been a present to him from the mother from whom as the children knew, he had for long been estranged. Although Jeremy was bitter against her, he frequently wore the brooch as an ornament in his most ornate satin cap which was also adorned by an upstanding bright feather.

It appeared that during the performance of the play the Queen noticed the brooch, and after the fall of the curtain she expressed her desire to speak with Jeremy and to see the ornament at closer range. He thereupon had plucked it from his cap and had handed it to her on his bended knee. As he told his wife afterwards, he was in mortal fear lest she should expect him to offer it to her, but although nobody appreciated a present more than Elizabeth, the donors were always of the wealthy nobility. In this instance, she at once realized that the brooch was of special, personal value to the handsome, gifted actor, and she was curious to know how he had come by it. She twisted it about in her hands which were, said Jeremy, the most exquisite hands he had ever seen on a woman, gazing at the intertwined initials H and J which were in rubies, and the diamond crown which surmounted them.

She asked Jeremy if he had any knowledge of the brooch's history, and he told her that years ago his mother had for a time been one of Queen Jane's attendants, and on the birth of the little Prince Edward, the brooch had been presented to her as a memento. His mother in her turn had, when he had come of age, given it to him as a hat decoration and as that he wore it.

The Queen had then said that she had seen more than one duplicate of the brooch, for they had been ordered by His Majesty King Henry VIII as gifts for his Queen's ladies. With nearly all these ladies the Queen had had some contact, but she had never heard of Mistress Grenton. She had enquired as to her maiden name, and Jeremy then explained that his father had adopted his mother's name on their marriage, which was the custom in their family when the estate passed to a female for lack of a male heir. As Annis Grenton, his mother had been Queen Jane's attendant.

Returning the brooch to him, Elizabeth had said that it was a precious heirloom and should be well guarded. Although she could not remember his mother, she had been very young at the time of her brother's birth and apparently Mistress Grenton had not been permanently attached to the Court. As an afterthought she had asked for the name and location of his mother's estate, and had instructed a courtier to write down the information. Pleasance, the Queen remarked, must be on the direct route to Lincoln which she had visited ere now and might haply visit again. She had dismissed Jeremy with much graciousness.

Robin and Lucy – they were never called by their more formal names – had listened to this with the greatest interest. They had often heard the Queen spoken of, and always with such awed admiration that to them she seemed more a being out of a fairy tale than an actual person. Robin asked if she was herself very beautiful, not only her hands.

'She has her own strange beauty,' his father answered, but his eyes had rested warmly on Joan, his wife, as though hers was the only beauty for him, as indeed it was.

A year after this the children had been orphaned, for although there was no major outbreak of the plague to send the theatre players out of London, never a year passed without exacting a toll of scattered victims. First Joan and then her husband fell grievously ill, and within a week both were dead.

The twins, with only the haziest knowledge that somewhere between London and Lincoln they had a grandmother, might have fared ill had it not been that Jeremy, with a presentiment when his wife sickened that time might be running short for both of them, consulted an attorney, giving him instructions as to the welfare of his children.

The kindly wives of other players cared for the twins until the attorney was able to communicate with Mistress Grenton who immediately sent four of her servants as escorts and the family coach itself to convey the two children to Pleasance. Money was also sent to Mr Pinner, the attorney, who was instructed to supply the children with mourning garments and to settle any debts Jeremy Grenton might have incurred.

So Robin and Lucy were carried away from London, and the world of players knew them no more. Robin carried his father's lute, and the white lace collar which relieved Lucy's black dress was fastened with the diamond and ruby brooch. Long ago her father had said that this brooch must be hers, because it was Robin who would presently have all else. At the time neither of the twins had understood what he meant, but they both remembered that Lucy was to have the brooch.

❋ CHAPTER 10 ❋

At the turn of the three-mile-long drive, Pleasance was revealed in all its beauty; an immense house with many windows upon which the setting sun glinted, bathing the entire mansion in a rosy glow. To Lucy, its towers and the twisted Tudor chimneys added a century ago to the original structure, seemed more of a castle than a house. Unprepared for such glory, her heart was twisted in a pleasurable yet agonized ecstasy as she gazed out of the coach windows. She was wide awake, though both children had slept little on the prolonged journey, but Robin in his corner was now deep in slumber.

The coach drew up with a fine flourish before the oaken entrance doors which it seemed to Lucy sprang open as though bidden to do so by a magic word. Within, she caught a glimpse of a great hall, and then pushing aside the footmen who emerged to open the carriage door, a tall, full-figured lady came swiftly down the flight of shallow stone steps, and uttered the children's names.

Lucy was the first to alight, but as the coach stopped, Robin awoke and uttered a distressful cry. Since his parents' death he had dreamt much of them and had grieved intensely for them, as Lucy had also grieved until the start of this journey when having so much that was new to look upon, she had been distracted.

The lady whom Lucy was sure was her grandmother took them both in her arms and still holding Lucy, bent to kiss away Robin's tears. 'Dear heart, you must not weep, not even for your father, on this the first time you see your own home,' Annis Grenton said. 'It is a joyous day.'

Poor Robin looked far from joyous as with an arm about them both their grandmother led them into the fairy-tale house. There was a fire in the great hall, for it was a chilly autumn evening. There were panelled walls, and rugs on a shining floor, and pictures in massive frames.

On that first evening their grandmother watched over them while a meal was served, and seemed content to gaze at them almost in silence. 'How unlike, though you are twins,' she murmured; a remark which they had both heard often enough and Robin, finding his voice, told her so.

'My brave boy, you have a great likeness to your father and to me,' said Annis, though she might have added that it was a watered-down likeness, for Robin was a frail-looking little boy. Lucy was different, and although it was her heir whom Annis had been most anxious to see, it was Lucy upon whom her eyes rested with a painful intentness; for here once again was the face that had been dearer to her than any face in the world; the dark, velvet eyes which were the facsimile of Nicholas Colton's, the slender, tall, lithe figure, the black, heavy hair, the olive skin and the finely chiselled mouth with its fugitive smile.

Could anything or anybody in the world, Annis wondered, have separated her from Jeremy had he borne such a resemblance to his adored father? As it was, she had loved her son, but with an imperfect love, discerning in him little of Nicholas but much of her wayward self.

That night saw the beginning of a new life which to Lucy at least was to be wholly pleasurable, for she soon shared her grandmother's adoration of Pleasance. Robin was delicate, and often ailing, and a cause for anxiety, but Lucy, for all that she remained thin and grew rapidly, rarely had so much as a cold.

Although Robin was the heir and they both now knew what their father had meant when he had told them he would have all, it was Lucy who proudly felt that she was a part of Pleasance and took a deep interest in everything that concerned it. For the past fifty years horses had been bred on the estate for sale, and it was through this private industry that Pleasance had chiefly prospered. Not only riding horses were reared and sold but also carthorses, for these were now gradually replacing oxen at the plough. An army of outdoor employees were kept fully occupied with this speciality, and Annis employed two bailiffs, one of whom was an old but still active and extremely knowledgeable man, whom she told Lucy had been trained over forty years ago by the Lady Grenton who had been her stepmother. There were acres of arable land belonging to the estate, some of which were ceded to sheep farmers who paid heavily for the privilege of grazing their stock.

Horses and the much-expanded dairy which not only supplied Pleasance with all its needs but sold its surplus in the local markets, were sufficient for their prosperity, Annis explained to Lucy, pleased by the child's vivid interest in every detail of the estate.

Robin spent far less time in the paddocks and stables, though he became better on horseback than his sister, who was never more than competent. Annis, herself an indifferent horsewoman, sympathized with this and she and Lucy frequently used the new family coach for outings. This was luxurious in comparison with the old springless vehicle which until ten or twelve years ago had been dignified by the name of coach.

One did not acquire a good seat on a horse by admiring the animals and being individually fond of them, said Annis, presenting Lucy on her thirteenth birthday with a pony already trained and disciplined to mildness. Robin, before this, had been given a colt, and rode it expertly without any particular affection for the animal.

The twins shared a tutor, but Robin was the more promising scholar. Lucy was fond of reading, but was bored by Latin and Greek and bad at figures. Annis's gaze would rest fondly on her as she sat reading. How like, how like, she would think with sorrowful pleasure, as Lucy with an impatient hand thrust back the thick, dark lock of hair which notwithstanding a confining cap persisted in straying across her forehead.

It was as well, said Annis, with a show of severity, that Pleasance would one day belong to Robin, for Lucy would never be concerned with the financial transactions which were so important, whereas these were already understood by her twin. But it was also well that Lucy had no jealousy of her brother, having already grasped that his sex made him the more important. One day she would, she supposed, marry and leave Pleasance, but as she explained to her grandmother, she felt that her very love for the estate made it partly hers, and she knew that whatever happened in the future she would be always welcome here.

'But that, madam, is a long, long way off,' said Lucy earnestly. 'You talk of yourself as old, but you do not look old, and it would not surprise me if you lived to be a hundred.'

'Then I should be famous indeed,' said her grandmother with a hearty laugh, 'and all the world would visit Pleasance to gain sight of me. But it is to be hoped that I do not keep Robin from his inheritance for such an unreasonable length of time.'

'Robin would be glad. He is very affectionate to people, even if the dear horses and dogs and Pleasance itself do not mean so much to him. He loves you, Grandmother, as he loved our parents.'

'Did you not love them?' Annis enquired curiously.

'Oh yes, indeed I did, especially my father, but not exactly in the same way. It is difficult to explain, but I have a narrow heart for love. Robin has not. He cares for the tenants, and our tutor, and the servants, and is upset when anything is wrong with them. He has the sense that they are part of him; that everyone is. That is the something of our mother in him . . . it was her nature. I remember hearing my father say so. She was so pretty and kind and sorry for all in distress. But sometimes,' Lucy ended, 'I think you are vexed when I speak of her.'

'No – not vexed, but I blame myself for my obstinacy,' said Annis, 'though in the end it was more your father's obstinacy than mine. I was angry when he loved your mother, and met her by stealth. Hard words passed between us. We both said more than should have been said. Your mother was the daughter of an actor in a company of strolling players who set up for a season in Mellor. Your father became vastly interested in the stage, and again and again rode over to Mellor to see the different plays. There he met your mother, who was with her father, and he fell in love with her. I could not believe he was serious in his wish to marry her; to me it was unseemly, and after one such quarrel he left Pleasance for which he had no great affection, and – I never saw him again. For many years I had no idea where he was, but in the last years of his life I heard he had become well known as a London actor, and I wrote – more than once. He did not reply, and I only knew that you and Robin existed after they were both dead.'

'He could not forgive you because you did not love my mother,' Lucy said. 'It was unreasonable, but then men are unreasonable.'

Annis said with amusement: 'You are young to have discovered that, though it went deeper with Jeremy than my disapproval of his wife. He did not wish to be drawn back to Pleasance. He thought of it not as a home of which to be proud, but as a prison. Though so unlike his father in appearance, Jeremy had something of his talents. Your grandfather was a scholar – a writer. He was versatile, and not only wrote and published an account of much that happened in the reign of Richard II, but wrote plays set in past history. One or two of them were performed by the students at the grammar school. I have thought since that Jeremy's talent for acting was an offshoot of his father's love of play-writing. My Nicholas, though he left London to live here and share my life, was never, I think, happy to be so far away from the great city. He indulged my wishes, he took my name and lost his own; he loved me and was endlessly good and unselfish, but Pleasance meant little to him. To me, the country and all concerned with it is life; to your grandfather it was stagnation and a kind of death.'

Annis sighed heavily as she uttered the last words, and Lucy was moved. She put her arm round her grandmother's neck and leant against her. 'I love it all,' she murmured, 'and Robin is not strong, and as he says feels so much better since he came to live here. Besides, I expect poets and musicians do their best work when they are rather solitary.'

'Is Robin both then?' enquired Annis. 'He has a pretty talent for the lute, I agree, and composes the songs he plays, but I had not supposed that the verses were also original.'

'They are, madam,' Lucy said eagerly. 'Sometimes at night he sits up until almost dawn, composing lyrics, and they are such sweet ones.'

'No wonder the boy looks heavy-eyed in the mornings,' was Annis's comment. 'As for poetry, I am no judge, though it seems that they all concern themselves with love and partings and roses.'

'Does it not seem though that Grandfather's talent has been transmitted to him, although it is I who more closely resemble him?'

'It may be so, though your grandfather was not musical, neither did he write verses.'

'Tell me about him,' coaxed Lucy. 'I love to hear about the time when you were young.'

'Oh child, when I look back, it is as though I remember another life.'

In her sixties, Annis Grenton was still a fine-looking woman, with her hair that showed little of grey, and a honey-cream skin. Her teeth were good, she had few wrinkles, and although her body was heavy, she carried herself with a straight back and squared shoulders. In her fashionable farthingale she was an impressive figure. Lucy, although not so readily affectionate as her twin, had become much attached to her.

'The time you spent at Hampton Court Palace must have been wonderful,' said Lucy.

In retrospect, after over forty years during which time she had not journeyed more than a few miles from Pleasance, it also seemed wonderful to Annis. As Lucy sat down on a stool beside her, near to the fire, she said : 'But you have heard it all before.'

'Only in bits and pieces. Was it not very exciting when Queen Jane stayed here?'

Lucy put her head down on the plump knees which, covered by several petticoats and a velvet skirt, made a comfortable pillow. Annis feeling more tenderly towards her than she had done to her own son, stroked the dark hair. As she described the events of so long ago Lucy listened raptly. It was strange and fascinating to hear her grandmother talk in a familiar way about the Princess Mary, and of the awesome King Henry, and of poor Queen Jane who had lived only a little over a week after the birth of the Prince, and had then lain for a whole fortnight in state at Hampton Court Palace, covered with a golden pall.

'They took her all the way to Windsor to be buried,' said Annis. 'But I escaped that, for your great-grandfather had fallen ill, and a message was sent to me to get permission to leave the palace. I don't know how I should have set about that. It was the Princess Mary, or the Lady Mary as she was then called, who arranged it for me. She was kindness itself in those days.'

'Why did she change so?' asked Lucy. 'She was a cruel Queen, and even when I was very small I heard all about the poor people she had ordered to be burnt alive because they were not Catholics. Even our Queen Elizabeth was in danger of losing her life.'

Annis shook her head with a perplexity she had often felt : 'I have never understood what happened to turn her to cruelty. It must have been those she had around her, to advise her, and to poison her mind against her sister; though it is true that when life goes awry for a woman, her whole nature can be twisted. All my memories of Queen Mary are otherwise.

66

She was but a girl then, but she had already suffered much. Queen Jane loved her, and when she died the Lady Mary mourned her sadly. I saw the little Prince's christening, and the Lady Mary held her sister by the hand, for she was so young, not much more than a baby. She used to play battle-dore and shuttle-cock with her in the long picture gallery at Hampton Court, and then to think that she had her put in the Tower and everyone believed she would order her head to be chopped off.'

'I suppose,' said Lucy thoughtfully, 'the King, her father, gave her that idea. She had been taught he could do no wrong, and that was the way in which he killed Queen Elizabeth's mother, and his other wife, Kathryn Howard.'

'Poor girl,' Annis said. 'It was a bad thing for her that the King's fancy fell on her. I had a terrible fear it would fall on me, when he looked at me one day and called me the Queen's Talisman. But it was no more than a pleasantry.'

'What did he mean by calling you a Talisman, madam?'

Annis hesitated. She had never told anyone except Nicholas of the Queen's fancifulness. She could not have said why it seemed to denigrate her, but it did; rather as though she had been brought to Court and received there in the same way that a King's jester was received, because he was a freak.

'She had a fantasy that I could give her strength because I was strong and she was delicate,' she said reluctantly. 'It was all an absurdity, but it amused your grandfather who thought I resembled the earth goddess, Ceres, though he called her Demeter.'

'But nobody has seen those heathen gods and goddesses; they don't exist; so how could he think you were like her?'

Lucy, who could sometimes be literal-minded, asked this question as Robin came in, and now Annis had two pairs of questioning eyes fixed upon her. The fair, pale boy in dark blue doublet and hose leant against the door he had closed, and gazed at her with the reflective expression that she found disconcerting.

'It was a foolishness, child,' she said. 'It was his imagination. I was tall and fair and strong, and I loved the country and all growing things; the very grass was sweet to me. I thought I could make him love it too, for he was so quiet and clever and wonderful in every way; but he seemed to fade with each year that passed. Once when we first knew each other, he said that he did not cling to life as I clung to it – try as I might I could not make him cling.'

'Was he very religious?' Robin asked.

'In his way, but not so as to cause trouble. When the Princess Mary became Queen, and it was dangerous not to be a Catholic, we went to Mass; but when our blessed Elizabeth came to the throne, then religion changed, and so did we, and most of the big families hereabouts. Your grandfather was relieved. He said that the Protestant faith was far less strain on credulity, and your father was brought up to be one; but these days there is great tolerance about beliefs. Your grandfather was vehement that should be so. At the time when Queen Mary reigned, he said that if any Protestants he knew were in danger, he would help them. It frightened me, and I was thankful that nobody ever came to him for help, for assuredly they would have been succoured here.'

'Hidden, do you mean?' asked Lucy. 'But where?'

'It seems now as though your grandfather was over-zealous to run into danger,' Annis said reluctantly, for even after so many years she would have been angered had these sharp-witted children ridiculed Nicholas. 'But when we heard of the burnings, which were not only in London, and many people were taking flight who had been informed against as Protestants, your grandfather employed workmen he could trust to panel the walls of the room in which Queen Jane had slept, the room which is now Lucy's. This panelling covered a powder closet which is as big as a small room, and when it was finished nobody could tell that the closet was beyond it. There is a secret spring; difficult to discover unless one knows where to look for it.'

Lucy was enchanted. 'A room leading off mine? Oh, madam, how exciting!'

'Silly child, it is no more than an extra-large cupboard that has never been used.'

'Yes, that's disappointing,' and Lucy sighed.

'It was no disappointment to me. I was always afraid that your grandfather's tolerance and sympathy might bring down trouble upon him. Truth to tell, I had forgotten about the secret room when I decided you should have Queen Jane's apartment as your own; it being large and airy and having a balcony and a fine view.'

'You have spoilt me,' said Lucy affectionately. 'Now I shall not rest until I have seen the little room behind the panelling and have been shown how to use the spring that opens the hidden door. You will show it to us, won't you?'

Robin added a plea to his sister's. 'We should know how to put such a room to use,' he said. 'One can never be certain. One day it may be needed.'

Annis derided this. 'Nonsense, boy, those bad times are over; none the less there shall be no secrets from you. How should there be, when one day Pleasance will be yours?'

'Why is it that some estates can be inherited by women as well as men?' asked Lucy. 'I wondered the other day when Mistress Rowser was here, and she said how hard it had been on Sir Hugh Derevale's daughters because although they all had families, Derevale Manor and the title had passed to a nephew.'

Annis who was vague about this, said it had something to do with the Salic Law, which did not always apply, for by that law property must descend through males. In the case of Pleasance, if there was no male heir, the estate automatically became the property of the nearest female heir. She thanked heaven that the title-deeds of Pleasance had never been in dispute, though in earlier days there had in some parts of the country been cases of estate-jumping. She added with a note of constraint in her voice that the owner of Pleasance could, if he wished, legally give his wife a life tenancy if she outlived him.

'That was so when your father died, madam, was it not?' Robin enquired. 'I have had several conversations with Mr Gettie, and with him went through the family archives; back to the time when Pleasance was first built. Mr Gettie said it would be strange indeed if I were not proud to be a Grenton; one of such a long and honourable line.'

'I trust that you are,' Annis said.

'Sufficiently so, I think, though it is almost a pity that Lucy and I cannot change places, for she says that if she ever leaves here, it will be as though the heart is torn from her.

Mr Gettie, who although he is not a lawyer appears to have much knowledge of the law, says he doubts if Lady Grenton could have established her claim to live here; that is if you had opposed her and brought a case against her, and this although he has a devotion to her memory, for it was she, he says, who first employed him when he was a very young man, as the assistant land-agent.'

'So she did.' Annis's still bright blue eyes had narrowed as she surveyed her grandson. 'My stepmother had great capabilities; she brought money into the family, and as my father was in poor health, much of the management of the estate fell to her. It certainly did not occur to me that I had the power to dispute the will . . . but I knew little of such matters. I was only a girl.'

'It could have made scant difference,' said Robin, 'as Lady Grenton lived for so short a while. Mr Gettie says that she pined away after great-grandfather's death, though it was hoped that the child she might have borne would have given her the wish to live.'

'This seems to have been a strange conference that you have had with Gettie,' Annis said, and with so much acerbity that both the children stared at her in astonishment.

Robin, with the grave young dignity that was natural to him, shook his head : 'No, madam, for you will recall that you advised me to study the family history because my father, who was so indifferent to it, had told me nothing.'

'That is true, but Lady Grenton was only connected with it through her marriage. She brought money to Pleasance, but did not live to bear a child who would only have been the heir had he been male.'

Lucy said dreamily : 'Poor Lady Grenton, she must have loved great-grandfather consumedly to be unable to live without him.'

Annis opened her lips to contradict, but closed them again with the words unsaid. It was as well, she concluded, that this should be the child's impression. Even now, after the passage of forty years, she recalled with shrinking the last months of her stepmother's life. At first the veiled triumph, and the pressure put upon her to consent to a betrothal with Sir Hugh Derevale; the scenes and the tears, and her stepmother's insistence that when her son was born, there would be no place for Annis at Pleasance.

These scenes had become less frequent as Lady Grenton's health deteriorated, but it had been a dark and frightening time; the pain, the sickness, the frequent visits from the apothecary; a pompous little man who had, Annis suspected, been also a vastly stupid one. Certainly no sinister suspicion had ever entered his mind, and until the last days of Isabel's life he had persisted that nothing was gravely wrong with her, that her sickness was natural, and due to her condition.

Never before nor since had Annis experienced such terror as in those days; a terror only augmented because she knew very little. Not a syllable had she and Susan exchanged about the pact they had made.

Was it a pact? Even now Annis could not be certain. She had faithfully kept her promise, and badly off Susan would have been, but for it, with a husband who had turned out to be a wastrel, a womanizer. Susan had had one baby after another who died in infancy, and her only living son, born when she was past forty, was said to be no better than his father.

But had Susan really *done* anything?

At the time Annis had wondered fearfully, but she had not asked Susan. She had not dared to ask her.

Isabel had died at last, after two days of unremitting sickness, and the apothecary had certified her death as heart failure brought about by the severity of her vomiting. Annis, by then, had been so worn out through sleepless nights and secret fear, that it had been easy to pretend grief. The neighbours had pitied the poor young girl overwhelmed by the calamity of losing both father and stepmother within the space of a few months. She had been a spectacle of lonely bereavement, and everyone had been good to her. None had suspected the passionate relief and triumph after Lady Grenton had been buried, and when Annis, surveying the domain, had known that it was hers.

She recalled how she had wandered from room to room, touching first one object and then another; the word 'Mine' constantly, silently reiterated. She had carried out an inspection ranging from cellars to attics; she had explored every

71

acre of the estate as though she saw it for the first time. Even now she could savour the intense satisfaction of those days, while she waited for an answer to the letter which she had sent to Nicholas.

She had never had a doubt of what that answer would be; but before they were married in the early spring, Susan had been wedded, and with the utmost thankfulness Annis had seen her depart from Pleasance.

One of her first actions had been to turn out an elderly couple from a cottage on the far edge of the estate. It had been a suitable cottage, and she had wanted Susan to be as far away as possible. The poor old couple, pensioners from Sir Lucian's day, were accommodated elsewhere, but nevertheless there had been much repining.

Susan had been jubilant. The new cottage was well furnished, and her Tam safely landed. Annis was praised for her generosity, though it had not been considered singular as Susan had been her personal maid.

Every year since then Annis had paid Susan an annual visit; a visit which she hated to this day, but otherwise they only saw each other by chance. Annis had been plain spoken. No reason was given, but she had forbidden Susan to visit her fellow servants at Pleasance.

Thinking of this, Annis moved her shoulders in distaste. The annual visit was now not far distant. She would drive there, and the bag of coins would change hands and Susan would offer her cakes of her own baking and a goblet of home-made wine. Annis would crumble the cake and sip the wine, and there would be the usual false, friendly converse; respectful thanks and gratitude from Susan; kindly condescension from Annis. Yet both would read the mind of the other. Susan's pebble eyes would pierce deep into Annis's thoughts, and she would be amused by the fear that was there. Scornful too, as she fingered the leather bag which contained the fifty gold pieces.

Annis had never taken these from the general fund. Instead, during the year, she saved coins out of the money she set aside to spend on herself. So much less to the mercer; to the shoemaker. It was better and safer, so she felt, for through this, nobody but Susan and herself knew of the transaction.

That Susan who had once been fond of her now despised her for the fear which sealed her lips, Annis did not doubt. Looking back, it seemed as though Susan did not know the meaning of fear.

This year, Annis decided, she would take Lucy with her on that hated visit. It would not be so bad with a third person present, especially a child who would not suspect undercurrents, and who would be interested in a new experience however ordinary and unexciting.

✻ CHAPTER 11 ✻

The years slid away as smoothly as a silk thread through the eye of an embroidery needle. The twins celebrated happy, uneventful birthdays, and when Robin was between fifteen and sixteen he went up to Oxford. Lucy missed him sorely, though her grandmother saw to it that she was well occupied; a lady of quality must be proficient in all domestic arts. How else could she instruct those of her household when she married?

A suitable marriage for Lucy was one of Annis's chief preoccupations. She allowed it to be known that her granddaughter would be well dowered, and by the time she was nineteen she had been approached by more than one personable suitor. But Lucy refused to consider any of them, and Annis remembered her own obduracy and would not press her unduly. It was Lucy's love of Pleasance that stood in the way, so Annis believed. She could not bear to think of marriage which would mean leaving it; though as Annis pointed out, when she died and Robin succeeded her, it might not suit Lucy to live there. In the natural way of things Robin would marry within a few years, and in due course his wife would be mistress of Pleasance. Could Lucy be happy under a sister-in-law's jurisdiction?

Lucy did not suppose she could, but insisted that it would be time enough to think of her marriage when Robin showed signs of an attachment.

Annis would have listened with less tolerance to such excuses had she guessed that in truth Lucy was no longer heart-whole, and had her plans which she hoped Robin might be induced to forward.

Two years before, when only seventeen, she had met Susan Reynolds' roving son, and the incident which had thrown them in contact, though it had greatly shaken Lucy, had been concealed from her grandmother.

While crossing the fields one bright summer morning, in preference to riding with a groom in attendance along the lane, a bull belonging to one of the tenant farmers had charged through a broken paling, and with down-thrust head had made for the terrified Lucy. The paralysed seconds in which she had stood helpless to move seemed the length of hours when she recalled them, and then with a shout, and stalwart, spread legs as he leapt the hedge, a tall figure had been between her and the savage beast.

Waving his jerkin as a flag, the man had distracted the creature, and with thrust and feint had finally succeeded in bewildering it. Shouts for aid had brought men running from the farmhouse and the bull had been secured, whereupon Lucy's rescuer had turned his attention to her.

She had thought then, in a dazed way, that he was a giant of a man, and indeed Stephen Reynolds was well over six foot in height and massively built. He was also more than passably prepossessing, with a bronzed, laughing face, sparkling brown eyes, and dark hair curling to his head. Lucy, herself, was of more than medium height, but beside him she felt as inconsiderable as a child.

Finding her rigid with fright he had reassured her and gentled her, much as she had seen a terrified horse gentled by a groomsman. She had not resented it. With shame, she had secretly admitted that she enjoyed it. When she was calmer he had taken her to his mother's cottage, and Susan had given Lucy a warm welcome, recognizing her not only from the visit she had paid with her grandmother years before, but because she had occasionally seen her since on her gentle, ambling mare.

Not a wit discomposed because he had rescued and afterwards fondled the young miss from the great house, Stephen

74

had looked at her with amused admiration, comprehending the shyness which had come upon her, but remembering the responsive warmth of trembling limbs when he had stroked them and murmured soothing words to her.

His mother was evidently proud of her handsome son, and Lucy had thought this touching. She realized that Susan must have been quite old when Stephen was born. He was the image of his father, Susan said, who had been just as big and strong and afraid of nothing. He had died when Steve was a toddler, and a great blank it had left in her life. Steve had been her comfort for many a year, but this quiet place was too dull and small for him, and to be a farmer was a dead way of life to his thinking. You couldn't hold back such a man, not when he was young, said Susan, and Steve had gone soldiering, and for six years had been away in foreign parts. He'd be off again in no time, for he had still another year to serve, and after that he might be ready to settle down. Meanwhile his old mother could keep the farm going with the aid of a couple of men who'd worked for her for years. Maybe in her old age Stephen would be near at hand.

Why Lucy had not told her grandmother of this adventure she could scarcely have said. It was as though she wished to cherish it in secret, and many a time during the next year she thought of that dark, audacious, smiling face, and remembered the touching of fondling hands.

There was nobody to tell her that Stephen Reynolds, as a boy, had been in every village brawl and later had caused a local scandal by an affair with a shopkeeper's wife. The result had been a child who had a striking likeness not to his ostensible father, but to the handsome Stephen. There had been a fight on the village green between husband and lover, in which the blameless one had come off the worst.

General disapprobation had been such that Stephen thought it wise to disappear from the locality, and by the time he returned, the shopkeeper was dead and his wife and children had left the district.

There were other stories, equally unsavoury, but how should they reach the ears of the shielded Lucy? So far as was known she had never even spoken to the reprobate, and certainly she was socially far removed from him.

Lucy learnt to be cunning, and Stephen was cunning by nature. Idling his time away with his army service over, he had time to spare, and Lucy had always roamed freely through the estate, though not beyond it without an escort. She rarely wanted to – there was the park and the little wood and the long drive, sufficient for exercise; providing also many a secret retreat.

From time to time Stephen was there waiting at some arranged meeting place, and if Lucy was not surprised because her virginity was still intact, that was the measure of her innocence, and the measure also of Stephen's self-control, which was based on self-interest and his mother's strictures.

'Get her with child, and you're undone, the pair of you,' said Susan, when she first became aware of their secret meetings. 'You don't know the ways of the quality as I do, or leastways the quality according to Mistress Grenton's notion of it. Miss Lucy's an innocent maid now, and she'll stay a maid until she marries you. That way there'll be her respect as well as her love, and she'll move heaven and earth to get you for her husband. She has a will of her own, quiet little wench though she is.'

'For that matter, so has Mistress Grenton,' Stephen retorted. 'And why you think she'll ever agree is a fair maze to me, though with a babe on the way there might be a chance. A bastard at Pleasance wouldn't be to her liking.'

'You girt fool!' Susan with her arms akimbo spat the words at him. 'D'ye think that hasn't happened before, to such as the Grentons? There's ways and means of getting rid of such whelps; farming them out or worse, and although Mistress Grenton has a fondness for the girl, she'd cast her out before she'd let scandal touch Pleasance. It won't be easy, mayhap, but you have a care with Lucy, and I'll do the rest. I wasn't her grandma's maid as went to Court with her and knew all her secrets for nothing.'

Stephen sitting astride a chair with his arms folded on the high back of it, looked at her curiously: 'There's some secret you hold over her,' he said slowly. 'D'ye think I haven't suspicioned it? Why for else would she pay you what she does, year after year? Cautious and secret too – not open as it could be, with you going up to the house to be paid your pension by the steward. I've held my tongue, but I've wondered.'

'Maybe you'll know one day, but it's to be hoped not . . . you who can't keep off the drink.'

Stephen laughed at his mother, as she turned away: 'Now, Mam, you know full well I can keep a still tongue, even when I'm in drink, and mayhap I'd drink little if there was something for me to do in this place, beyond milking a few cows and the like. That's no life for a man, and if it hadn't been for Lucy, and for you saying we'd the chance of getting wed, I'd have been right off again . . . to sea, this time; one of Drake's men maybe.'

'Where's this roving life getting you?' Susan demanded. 'There'd be plenty for you to do at Pleasance if you took over when old Gettie gives up, as he must before long. He's past his three-score. You've turned thirty-two, Steve, and it's time you settled. The young master's a scholar; a pretty boy with his white fingers and his lute and his verses, but you're twice the man he'll ever be, and as I heard said at Court years ago, it's the power behind the throne that rules. You bear what I say in mind and have a care. I'll give the word when you're to speak up and tell Lucy the time has come to ask Mistress Grenton for her in marriage.'

'That'll be a day for the fine lady,' Stephen remarked sardonically. 'Lucy hasn't said a word to her; not even told her when I stepped between her and Barker's bull near two years ago.'

Susan said thoughtfully: 'It was odd she didn't. There was nothing in that to hide.'

Stephen smiled, the mocking smile which resembled his mother's, though lighting his fine eyes and curving his full lips, it was attractive, not repellent.

'Nothing to my way of thinking, but something to hers. I cuddled her a bit.'

Susan looked at him and laughed. But then she said seriously: 'You're a fine one, your father over again, and a mint of trouble he caused me before he turned up his heels. Mad though I was for him when I wed him, it was no grief to me to be a widow. If you've a mite of sense, you'll have a care when you marry Lucy. You'll work hard to better yourself, and make yourself of value at Pleasance, and you'll treat her well and with respect, so that she can still hold up her head, even though folks will say she's married beneath her. You've got a fine chance, Steve, and that 'ull be owing as much to me as to your looks and ways which have won the girl over to you. For all her gentle eyes, there's a hard strain in Lucy, and I'm warning you.'

'Warning me of what? I shan't beat her, as the old man beat you at times.'

'There's other ways of making a girl feel she's had enough of marriage,' said Susan. 'If only you'd got as much sense as you have good looks. There's not more than one man in ten who's faithful to his wife, but there's many wives who are none the worse for it, because they never know it.'

Stephen shrugged. He said : 'You warn me about that later on, Mam. Taken with her as I am, it's her I want, and no other wench, but I haven't got her yet.'

'You will,' said Susan.

✳ CHAPTER 12 ✳

In the year 1593 the Queen was sixty, but from the odes composed in her honour, one might have supposed she was in the first flush of radiant youth. The great nobles with large country estates vied with each other to devise extravagant masques and pageants in her honour, and undeterred by advancing years, the Queen with her entourage graciously consented to leave London in order to be thus entertained.

The Earl of Leicester who had been her favourite for many years had died shortly after the defeat of the Spanish Armada, but his place had been taken by Robert Devereux, Earl of Essex, then in his late twenties. He it was who was nearest to the Queen on all her travellings and it was for him, as much as for her own gratification, that the Queen made a great effort to preserve her looks.

Returning from a visit to Nottingham, the Queen suddenly bethought herself of the young actor, Jeremy Grenton, who ten years before had knelt before her, proffering his ruby and diamond brooch composed of the initials H and J for her inspection. Although the royal memory was said to be fault- less, in this instance it was probably jogged by the fact that an old play by Lyly had been produced for her amusement, and it was in this play that she had seen Jeremy act a leading part.

The Queen remembered that his family estate was on the route to London. Thereupon, she caused enquiries to be made, and heard to her regret that the handsome Jeremy had died some years ago, but that his mother, whose identity had provoked her curiosity, was still living on her country estate with her two grandchildren.

The Queen's mind often lingered on the past; especially on the years when her father was king. To her he had per- sonified greatness. He was not the monster that some of his subjects judged him to be. He was terrible, but he was majestic. He was unpredictable, sometimes teasing, tender and loving, sometimes the being who held her life in his hands. He could have commanded her death as easily as he had com- manded poor Kathryn Howard's, and her own mother's. On Anne Boleyn of whom she never spoke, Elizabeth's thoughts often rested in an agony of pity.

She had never tried to understand her father's actions, for they were beyond understanding, but they had made her realize how terrible it was for a woman to deliver herself with love into any man's hands. She thanked her God that she had never loved sufficiently for that.

Jane had succeeded in anchoring Henry's affections, but would she have done had she lived? The Queen flogged her memory, conjuring up from her long-past childhood a gentle face and a quiet voice. Only a dim memory, but Mistress Grenton must have a clearer one.

With this in mind, Elizabeth sent a message to announce that the royal entourage would stop at Pleasance for a few hours on the homeward journey. Mistress Grenton, she said graciously, was to make no untoward preparations for her, as it would be but a brief visit.

The message threw Annis into a whirlwind of confusion. It was impossible not to make preparations, even though the Queen might be there for only a few hours. The message

79

had said that she did not intend to sleep there, as after the slight detour she would press on towards Oxford. But who could tell that she might not change her mind, thought Annis, resolved that the best rooms should be garnished against the chance of an alteration in the schedule.

With only three days to accomplish much, every soul on the estate was pressed into service. The tent which had been set up for the twins' last birthday was once more erected and adorned with gilt hangings. Long tables were spread with every conceivable delicacy, for calling upon her resources, and with two days given up to baking and roasting and all the culinary arts, Annis could achieve much. The great dining-room was prepared, decorated with the flowers the Queen was known to admire, and the family glass and gold plate brought out from coffers where some had been hidden away for years.

Robin was summoned from Oxford; Lucy, in an apricot-coloured silk-damask gown which was highly becoming to her, was hung about with Annis's pearls and told to wear the royal brooch. Various notabilities were invited to meet the Queen.

It was the most exciting event in local history, and although few would have wished to undertake such preparations in so short a time or to have had such expenditure thrust upon them, Annis was yet greatly envied.

As the hour for the Queen's arrival approached, Robin on a splendid roan horse headed the procession which rode out from Pleasance to greet her, and to escort her up the long drive to the main entrance.

The usual royal escort gave place to this cavalcade, and the Queen was seen to smile with pleasure on the fair, delicately handsome lad who looked less than his nineteen years. On the steps Annis, rejuvenated by excitement, tall and regal, waited with Lucy to receive the Sovereign. Her greengage-coloured satin gown was rich, her diamonds which had once belonged to Isabel Grenton were fine stones if in old-fashioned settings. Pleasance, so dearly loved, and for many years the object of almost fanatical care and devotion, had never looked more charming. Although by the standards of great estates it was relatively small, it had a cameo-like perfection with its emerald lawns, noble trees and masses of flowering bushes, and the Queen gazed around her with gracious appreciation.

What a fortunate thing it was, thought Lucy, that she and her grandmother had dressed in brilliant colours, for the Queen was in white, and her coach was of silver, upholstered in white. It was hard to realize that she was no longer young, hard indeed to realize that she was an actual woman and not a moving effigy.

Her long oval face was colourless, her torso in its tight, straight, jewelled bodice was flat, and the fashionable ruff concealed her throat, as did the tight sleeves her arms. Beneath a small, white hat with a silver plume and a diamond buckle, her wig was of dark, silky red. Her brows were so faint that they were scarcely discernible, but the hooded eyes were bright. Those eyes, and her hands from which she presently withdrew gloves sewn with pearls, were the only real things about her, Lucy thought, wondering how she could on this warm day, endure the discomfort of such close, stiff garments.

To the fascinated Lucy she seemed unearthly; the hands, loaded with rings, were white and exquisite and could have been the hands of a girl. When the right hand was extended to Lucy and she knelt to kiss it, it was as cool as a snowflake. The Earl of Essex hovered at the Queen's side, and although he was a handsome young man, and she an old woman, he appeared to adore her. Lucy, strange to say, credited him with sincerity. It would not be difficult to adore the Queen as one might adore a goddess.

At the repast which followed, the Queen ate and drank sparingly, but the members of her entourage more than atoned for that. They made merry in the big tent, dispensing with etiquette when the Queen and her intimates were within the house.

After the repast, Robin played his lute, and sang verses of his own composition extolling the Queen's majesty. As they had been composed at top speed within the last twenty-four hours, they were not of his best, but he had a sweet tenor voice and the Queen, sitting in a tall-backed chair, leant her elbow on one arm of it and cupped her cheek in her palm, bending slightly forward to listen to him.

Robin compared the Queen to Cynthia, the goddess of chaste

moonlight; compared the effulgent beam of her eyes to these silver rays. Such lyrics must have been composed many times, but the sweetness of Robin's voice gave them distinction. In a moved voice the Queen praised and thanked him, and then turning to Annis engaged her in conversation. At a gesture from her the others fell back, even the Earl of Essex.

To Annis the Queen spoke of Queen Jane, and told her that years ago, having questioned her son Jeremy about the royal brooch he was wearing, she had had the curiosity to make enquiries about Annis's sojourn at Hampton Court Palace when the little Prince Edward was born.

There had been one lady, retired from Court, but much esteemed in her old age, who had greatly loved Queen Jane and remembered Annis. This lady had said that Queen Jane in her weakness had believed that Annis possessed some source of primitive strength which was communicated to her. It was a delusion, doubtless. With a sigh, the Queen remarked that she wished it could have been the truth. So much tragedy might have been avoided had the Queen lived. She had had a tender influence upon the King, and also upon the Princess Mary. Both of them had often spoken of it. Had Queen Jane lived, she might not have changed the course of destiny, for the little Prince was too delicate to attain to manhood, and she might have had no other children; 'But I,' the great Queen said, 'should have come to the throne under happier auspices. As a child I loved my sister Mary, and she loved me . . . it was not my love that ceased.'

Annis, startled by this strange confidence, did not venture to make any comment, and Elizabeth went on to speak of other matters which were not revealed to Lucy until after the departure of the royal visitor. Then, with a solemn face, Robin told her that the Queen having been taken, he supposed, by his singing and lute-playing and versifying, had commanded him to attend upon her at Court. He was to present himself at Greenwich Palace within the next few days.

'Don't look so downcast,' Robin rallied Lucy. 'It is but a fancy, and no doubt Her Grace will soon tire of me and require me no further. 'Tis little more than a gracious impulse to honour our family. If by any chance I do stay for more than a few weeks, I shall entreat the Queen to extend her favour to you. You might even find a gallant there for a husband, being too fastidious to choose any local squire.'

Robin laughed, because Lucy blushed, and had no idea that the blush was one of guilt. He would, Lucy knew, think her far from fastidious if he discovered that she was in love with Stephen Reynolds, whose mother had been a servant at Pleasance, though Annis's bounty had raised her above her station.

Stephen, through his years of wandering and with his fascinating knowledge of foreign countries, seemed to be of no particular class. He was utterly different from the other villagers who touched their forelocks to Lucy when she passed. But would her grandmother or her brother ever see him as she saw him? In order to marry, they would have to elope, and to elope meant leaving Pleasance. If she did, would they be forgiven?

Susan Reynolds had hinted that Stephen was fully qualified to step into old Mr Gettie's place when he retired, and he should have retired before now. He was too old and feeble to act as a land steward. The suggestion, carefully implanted, had given Lucy hope. Also, the old woman had flung out the information that Lucy's own great-grandmother had been of no more worldly account than Stephen. But Sir Lucian Grenton had loved her and married her. Why should not history repeat itself? Lucy pondered.

Stephen, when questioned, had professed his willingness to settle down for her sake. Adventure beckoned and the famous Drake was ready to take on men of Stephen's calibre, prepared to sail the seas, and share the excitement of discovering unknown lands to colonize; but Lucy, so Stephen protested, meant more to him than adventure, and he sympathised with her passionate love of Pleasance.

She need never leave it, he insinuated, if he stepped into old Gettie's shoes. There was the Dower House which had not been used for generations, though it had been kept in a good state of repair. Why should that not be given over to them if they married and he was the land steward? Lucy, then, would still be living on the estate and almost within sight of the great house.

To a girl sunk fathoms deep in infatuation, that was a blissful picture. Day by day she came nearer to plucking up her courage. Again and again she promised herself that she would make full confession to her grandmother before night-fall, only to shirk this when she was alone with Annis and given the opportunity.

CHAPTER 13

In the end it was not Lucy who revealed the truth to her grand-mother, but Mistress Foster, the parson's wife, who on a round of visits to the more humble parishioners, chanced, being pressed for time, to take a short cut through the wood on the border of the Pleasance estate. There to her horror, she came upon Lucy in the embrace of the ne'er do well Stephen Reynolds, whom the good lady only knew by sight as he was not wont to favour the village church with his attendance. Within hours, Annis was informed of her grand-daughter's perilous association.

Challenged by the dumbfounded Annis, Lucy defiantly de-clared that she was in love with Stephen, and wished to marry him, and for the first time she knew what it meant to receive the full brunt of her grandmother's anger. Having slapped Lucy on either cheek for her impudence, Annis stormed at her disgraceful behaviour. She was sent off to her own room and locked in there. Afterwards, a written message was sent to Susan, demanding her attendance. She was not to be accom-panied by her son, Annis wrote, for they would settle the business between them.

There was not the slightest doubt in Annis's mind that this could be accomplished. There was little that money was unable to do, though she was furious with Lucy for the neces-sity. Mistress Foster had already solemnly vowed that not a word should pass her lips, and in return Annis had promised that a large and anonymous subscription towards 'church expenses' should be sent to her husband. She only hoped Lucy's indiscretion was unsuspected by anyone else, but judged that had others been aware of these secret meetings she would have been told of it.

When Susan arrived, riding in state in one of the farm carts that had been sent for her, she stalked undismayed into the room where Annis was waiting to receive her. This was the library, rarely in use nowadays, though Nicholas had made it especially his during his lifetime.

Although the time for disclosure was not of Susan's choosing, she had little regret that it had come about. She could not have held Stephen in check for much longer. Bored with a long-drawn-out courtship he would either, she concluded, have seduced the girl or, had he given up hope of marrying her, would have gone off again on his wanderings.

Lucy's bedroom window looked out upon the drive, and when she saw Susan descend from the wagon drawn by two carthorses, she could well imagine what her grandmother had in mind. Susan would be admonished and probably bribed, perhaps threatened with expulsion from her home if she did not immediately put an end to the love affair.

Lucy's heart plunged in despair. Although she had every faith in Stephen, she could not expect him to sacrifice his aged mother. Susan Reynolds was dependent on the mistress of Pleasance who had all the power. As much, thought Lucy, over that which took place on her domain as the Queen had over her Court. There might have been a chance for her had Robin been at home for he was completely unworldly and only wanted to see her happy. He might have interceded for her and induced their grandmother to relent; in fact Lucy had contemplated telling him about her love for Stephen. Robin, after all, was the heir, and if he championed her it would carry weight.

Now she was only conscious of an agonized helplessness and began to sob hysterically. She was a prisoner and could not release herself. If she attempted to climb out of the window she would probably be killed, for there was a drop of many feet beneath her balcony, and if she fell it would be upon paving-stones.

She rushed to the door and senselessly shook it, hammered with her clenched fists upon it, and then drew in her breath with a gasp as she heard a slight tinkling noise on the parquet without. She realized that although her grandmother had locked her in her room she had not withdrawn the key which through the belabouring on the door had fallen out of the lock to the floor.

Where had it fallen? There might be just a chance . . .

Lucy dropped to her knees and then lay flat on her stomach as she peered beneath the narrow line of the door. There, only a few inches away, she could see the brass key. Could she draw it towards her, and if she could, would there be room to pull it through beneath the edge of the door?

Amongst various jewels she owned a pin with a gold and amethyst head which could be put to more than one use. Sometimes it fastened her fichu; sometimes it helped to confine the great roll of her dark hair. Its importance to her now was that the pin was long.

She got up and found it, and then there were several tantalizing minutes during which she endeavoured to edge the key towards her. It slipped and skidded on the parquet floor without, and once she thought that she had pushed it far away; but then her eagerly peering eye saw that it had but slipped into a horizontal position and that made it easier to guide. At last she had the key pushed close against the outer side of her door, but the pin was not enough to pull it through to her, and in desperation she thought of using her scissors to cut away a shaving of the door itself.

This proved to be unnecessary, though the scissors were useful, for with their blades she was able to grip the ring at the end of the key, and to drag it under the edge. The patience she had employed had steadied her, and she was no longer hysterical as she gazed at her prize. It was now the work of a second to unlock her door and to step out into the passage.

She had no idea where her grandmother would be interviewing Susan Reynolds, and she decided that she would go from room to room until she discovered them together. If her grandmother had locked the door she would be forced to let her in, for if she did not, she would cause a commotion. As it chanced her first guess was the correct one. She had thought that the library, only occasionally used when Annis conferred with her land agent, would probably be the most suitable for an unpleasant interview, and softly turning the handle of the door and finding it unlocked she slipped within.

Hanging before the door on its inner side there was a heavy tapestry curtain which Lucy had helped to work. She stood fingering it, at first aware only of the hum of voices, her heart thundering so loudly in her ears that she was unable to distinguish the words; and then after a few minutes, as she became calmer, these were clear to her :

'Well, name your price,' said Annis with a cold arrogance which Lucy had seldom heard her employ. 'I have already told you to dismiss any hope of my compliance. Nothing you have said or could say would bring that about, but in such cases as these a peaceable settlement is desirable. What will your son take or what will you take on his behalf? My sole condition is that he leaves the neighbourhood within the next twenty-four hours, and does not return here until my granddaughter has made a suitable marriage.'

'It's a hard condition, Mistress—hard on me as well as upon Stephen. He's spent too many years away from me, and he's all I have to be the comfort of my last days.'

If Annis's voice was arrogant, Susan's was whining. Lucy ventured to peep round the edge of the curtain, and saw the two women sitting opposite to each other, on either side of the big desk. How old, how terribly old they looked, was her first thought. And of course they were, for they were both in their seventies. Susan must be nearing eighty. Yet both were so vigorous, and made so few concessions to age, that that had never before impressed itself upon Lucy. Now, Susan, as she bent across the table, tapping it with a bony finger, looked wizened, and her expression was malicious. Annis sat upright, but her ruddy cheeks were mottled, her eyes screwed up into narrow slits, and her lower lip thrust forward in anger.

'His banishment,' said Annis, 'may not be for over long. My first concern will be to see Lucy under the care of one who can be trusted to look after her. She has had several offers of marriage which in my weak fondness I have permitted her to reject, but there will be no more of that. Lord Haybrill has only recently offered for her, though she knows nothing of it, for I and her brother considered him too old and dour, and were loth that she should go as far away from us as Haybrill in Lancaster : but now his lordship's very sobriety and the seclusion in which he lives will be an advantage, and also the distance . . .'

Lucy barely repressed a gasp of horror. She had seen Eustace, Lord Haybrill, several times when he had been visiting in the neighbourhood. He had been invited to dine at Pleasance, and she had thought him dreadful; a dark, thin, hook-nosed man, with a sneering mouth and an appraising eye which as it passed over her had filled her with apprehension. Surely, oh surely, her grandmother could not be serious?

'That,' said Susan, 'would be a cruelty, a worse cruelty than the match her ladyship had in mind for you, years ago. You married the man of your choice, so what's to be said against it if your granddaughter takes after you?'

Annis trembled with rage as she retorted : 'The case is completely different. Lady Grenton was my stepmother and she hated me; also there was nothing that anyone could bring against my chosen husband who was a fine and blameless gentleman. Your son has acted badly by me, Susan, but as he *is* your son whom you love, I have no wish to hurt you by speaking my mind about him. You are not ignorant. You know his reputation.'

Susan uttered a scoffing laugh : 'He's no worse, and better mayhap than many a handsome fellow with all the women after him. He's got a way with him, has Steve; he's different from the oafs who've never set foot away from here. Your lass is the same as all others, and was from the minute she clapped eyes on him. She's warm to marry him. And what's odd about that? Didn't Sir Lucian marry a girl who was no more quality than my Steve? Didn't your son do the same, and the quarrel over it cost you sore? It's in the blood, Mistress, and for all your pride there's naught you can do to alter the way of things.'

'There's much I can do,' uttered Annis between clenched teeth.

'That's foolishness and you know it; but why take it so hard? When we was girls we was fond of each other. A scared little rat you were, and I was sorry for you. I helped

you, didn't I? It's time you remembered it. But for me, you
likely wouldn't be as you are now. If her ladyship's wain
had been a boy, you'd have lost Pleasance for good and all.
It's through me there was no wain, and that her ladyship
didn't live long to keep you from your rights.'

'Be quiet!' Annis hissed.

'Such a fuss about it all,' Susan said, sinking her voice
to a wheedling note. 'Make the best of it, Mistress. My Steve
could take over old Gettie's job tomorrow and do well in it.
He and Lucy could set up together at the Dower House,
they . . .'

Annis broke in violently: 'Never. Better that Lucy were
dead and coffined. Defy me over this, and I'll turn you out
with not a penny piece. For over forty years you've lived
here by my grace and favour on the farm I ceded to you.
Your man was a no-good, and you'd have starved or been
out to work again but for the money you got from me each
year. I've done enough and more for you, and unless this
business is put to an end I'll see you rot in the gutter and
not raise a finger to prevent it. Tell your son that: tell him
he'll bring ruin upon you and tell him that's my last word.'

'Not quite your last,' said Susan.

By this time, Lucy was so caught up in the strange drama
that she had almost forgotten she was the cause of it. She
dropped the curtain and stepped into the room. Susan saw
her from out the corner of her eye, but Annis did not turn
her head.

'There's little,' said Susan, 'that can be done to me that
matters at my age; and Steve, before the law came down on
me, would be off and away; I'd see to that. Maybe, I'd save
my neck by turning evidence against you. After all, what
was I but a poor, ignorant girl who didn't know what was
being planned? I was no more than your tool – yours and
the fine, clever gentleman you married who maybe put you up
to it. Young though you was you'd got education, and you'd
got reason to want to see the end of her. Maybe as time went
on and I understood how I'd been used by you my conscience
began to fret at me; natural enough as I'm old and can't
have much longer to live. That I've something to lose I don't

deny, but you, Mistress, have more. All I've got to do is to go to Master Truelove, him who's a Justice of the Peace, and make my confession and then where would you be, my fair lady, and where would your son's children be?'

Annis's colour had deepened until it was almost purple. 'You're mad,' she cried. 'You can prove nothing. From first to last it was your doing. I was never even sure that you had done anything to help kill her. You took it into your own hands, and afterwards when she was dead I couldn't bear the sight of you, it horrified me. I forbade you even to come to the house again, though I kept my word to you.'

'Yes, you kept your word,' agreed Susan. 'And what's more you wrote it down, and so wasn't able to get out of keeping it.'

'You made me before anything happened. I never understood why; or at least . . .'

'Not until she was dead and no babe was born; then you remembered and pulled your wits together. We was both in it, and well you knew it when you told me that after what had happened you'd lose your reason if you had to see me about the place. Not that I cared as I'd got my man and a farm of my own.'

At that moment, Annis turned her head and saw Lucy. 'You! How did you get out? How long have you been there?' she demanded harshly.

Susan gave an evil chuckle. 'Long enough, Mistress. I saw the wench though you didn't, and as you were threatening me I didn't warn you. It's time she knew the truth of things. Being no dullard she must have already pieced 'em together, and if she hasn't, belike the paper you signed will help her.'

A long, gnarled hand was thrust into the front of a shabby bodice, and a square of parchment still stiff enough to rustle was pushed beneath Lucy's eyes. She bent to read the writing on it – Annis's writing – which had changed little with the years.

'I promise Susan Partridge that when I am the owner of Pleasance, I will give her . . .'

Lucy read no more, for the paper was snatched from her. Annis caught it up and held it clenched in her hands. 'I should have got this from you and destroyed it long ago,' she cried.

Susan moved round the table towards her. 'You give it up,' she said threateningly. 'Tear it or burn it, and there's naught will keep my mouth closed. As for you, my lass, it's time you knew my fine lady for what she is, bribing a poor ignorant girl to do away with her stepmother and the babe unborn that 'ud have turned her out of Pleasance.'

Lucy glanced from Susan's menacing face to Annis's twitching one. She was horrified and sickened, but all her loyalty rose up to defend her grandmother.

'That's all nonsense. I don't believe a word of it,' she said stoutly. 'You are in a delirium. Give her the paper, Grandmother. Let her do her worst. Nobody in their senses would believe her.'

'No.' Annis got out the one word with difficulty.

'Some will believe and some won't,' said Susan. 'But if one believes, there'll be mischief done. You fool, Lucy— it's for you and Steve that I've turned on her. You'll never get him but for me, and what I hold over her head.'

'Stephen won't allow you to do any such thing,' Lucy retorted. 'We love each other, and we'll find our own way out of this . . . Grandmother, please, the paper . . .'

With resolution she endeavoured to disengage Annis's clutching fingers, but old as she was, Annis was still sufficiently strong to prevent her. For a moment Susan watched them with an evil, sardonic amusement, and then went to Lucy's aid.

As she felt Susan's bony hands on hers, Annis shuddered and uttered a choking cry. 'It was the toad . . . you were like one . . . your hands are now . . . they're as dead and cold,' she cried, and then struggling and gasping for breath, she collapsed in Lucy's arms.

Unprepared, and not strong enough to hold the weight of the heavy body, Lucy staggered back and Annis fell to the floor. She lay there, unconscious but breathing stertorously.

Above the heaving body, Lucy gazed at her lover's mother with horror and disgust. Susan got down on her knees, and peered at the unconscious Annis. ''Tis an apoplexy,' she said. ''Twas the shock of you struggling with her. Me, I had no hand in it. I call God to witness that I had no hand in it. She sent for me and she threatened me. Nothing would do for her but to come between you and my lad, and I was fighting for you.'

'The fight is over,' said Lucy.

CHAPTER 14

Annis Grenton died without recovering consciousness, though to Lucy who watched beside her, it seemed as though she well knew what was going on around her, and would have spoken if she could.

Lucy was certain that her grandmother's eyes pleaded with her, and she had no doubt what they asked. It was an entreaty which could be answered in only one way. She knelt beside Annis and held both her hands. 'Be at peace,' she said. 'I will not marry him. I promise you.'

A messenger rode off to London to bid Robin return to Pleasance, but he did not arrive there until the next day, and by then it was too late. Annis was dead.

Lucy, exhausted after a night's vigil, had little to tell him. She had already decided that he must not know the truth. She did not for a moment believe that Susan Reynolds would utter a word. She would have nothing to gain from it. The girl she had coerced years ago – had she coerced her? was now beyond her power. If she told her story of poison and death she would be rated as a madwoman, and Robin, if threatened, would be incredulous.

But how could Susan threaten effectively now when the promise that Annis had written down and signed was in Lucy's possession?

Lucy had conceived a shuddering horror of this paper and would not even glance at it, but she realized its importance. Her grandmother might have destroyed it, but Lucy did not dare. For all she knew, if any future slander were uttered about Annis, the promise written on this paper might absolve instead of telling against her. Surely it could be reasoned that no girl lending herself to a murderous scheme would put such words on paper? To Susan Reynolds they might be evidence of complicity but not to anyone else.

So Lucy argued, her mind in a tangle of grief and loss and disgusted horror; not horror of her dead grandmother, but of Susan Reynolds. The evil old woman had also caused Annis's death, and because of her it had become unthinkable to marry Stephen.

Her grandmother, thought Lucy, must surely have known that, though her eyes had begged for reassurance. A girl might love a man intensely, but love and marriage could not unite under such circumstances. She was now forced to turn aside from Stephen, to behave as though he had never existed, to forget him as many a sorrowful girl had been forced to forget a dead lover.

That being so, there was no reason why Robin should be told anything of the scene which had brought about their grandmother's death. Lucy no longer needed him as an ally.

The servants knew nothing, and so could not gossip. It might have been thought strange that old Susan Reynolds had been bidden to Pleasance when that had not happened before, but that she was in any way the cause of their mistress's death would not occur to anyone. There remained only Mistress Foster, the parson's wife who had seen Lucy with Stephen, but she had promised to keep silent, and if Robin would carry out his grandmother's promise to send her husband a subscription to be used for any purpose he chose, she would doubtless be as good as her word.

But what of the paper, whether incriminating or otherwise? What could she do with it? She would be afraid to keep it amongst any of her belongings. It was then that she thought of the secret room beyond hers which Robin and she had explored since Annis had told them about it. Both of them knew how to manipulate the hidden spring, and Lucy, fascinated by the small, dark chamber which had no window, but received sufficient air from a fireplace with a wide, draughty opening, had insisted on furnishing it with a rough table and a couple of chairs. At the time when they were first told of the secret room, the twins had been young enough to use it as the setting for games, pretending by turns to be prisoner and gaoler. It was a private play known only to their indulgent grandmother. Now Lucy decided that the ominous paper could well be hidden there, and hidden it was; safe from prying eyes but where she could put her hand upon it if she needed it.

In the melancholy days that followed Annis lay in state, and those employed at Pleasance, as also Robin and Lucy, took their turns at praying by her bier. Lucy was astonished but soothed to see the change that death had wrought in her grandmother's countenance. With the lines smoothed from her face, Annis looked years younger. One could remember her thus, rather than in the furious rage which had caused the fatal apoplexy.

Stephen Reynolds was amongst the crowd of villagers who attended the funeral. Susan was mute, and he had no idea of the circumstances which had brought about Annis's death, though he had a strong suspicion that his mother's commanded visit to Pleasance had had something to do with it. She had been sent home in the wagon which had conveyed her to the great house, and had told Stephen that while she was there the mistress of it had been taken ill. For days Susan seemed shaken, and she did not go to the funeral. She was too old, she said, herself too near her death, but once the last ceremony was over she revived somewhat and insisted that the way was now open to Stephen. Lucy Grenton loved him, and her brother was a weakling, and would not for long last out against their marriage; not if the lovers were strong enough.

With Robin now lord of Pleasance, Lucy for the time being was mistress. The servants took their orders from her, and Robin gave her full authority. She had never loved Pleasance as much as she did in those days, and her frequent thought was that she could not bear to be separated from it. It was as though all her grandmother's obsessive devotion to the estate had been joined with hers. This, perhaps, was accounted for by the fact that her authority and importance were likely to be of short duration, for Robin after a decent interval returned to London.

The Queen wished to retain Robin at Court, and had, so he told Lucy, half-promised to revive his great-grandfather's title and to bestow it upon him. That, it seemed, was an honour Robin coveted, but Lucy suspected he was also drawn back to London by a romantic interest which he had partially confided to her.

It was vested in the Honourable Aurora Fernand, a wealthy orphan who was one of the Queen's maids of honour. She was, Robin said, different from other girls. Not exactly beautiful, but wise and gentle. Her mother had been a French lady who had died giving birth to Aurora, and the child, at the request of her mother's family, had been educated in France. At seventeen with her education completed, Aurora's father had sent for her to come to England, and had besought the Queen with whom he was in favour to look kindly upon her.

That Elizabeth had promised to do, and when she made a promise she took it seriously. Aurora's father was in ill-health, and did not live for long after the Queen took his daughter under her care; since when Aurora had been so strictly chaperoned that it was far from easy for any man to pay court to her.

Aurora loved the Queen who treated her with tenderness but as she might have treated a child, which was absurd as she was now eighteen, said Robin. He was strongly attracted to her, and it seemed to be mutual, since Aurora met him by stealth as often as she could.

Robin was not yet twenty, but he was steadfast as Lucy knew. It was unlikely he would change, and the Queen could not for ever deny Aurora the right to marry. Although she was an heiress, there was nobody who could say that Robin with his fine estate and his attractive presence and disposition was not a suitable match for her.

Lucy strove to force the thought of Stephen from her mind, which was not overwhelmingly difficult; a fact that puzzled her. She did not realize she had been shocked out of love, but felt that the upheaval she had suffered on his account could have happened in another lifetime. But she was not surprised that he made several attempts to see and speak to her. He was even bold enough to write a letter to her and leave it at the house, where Lucy found it amongst a pile of others sent by local acquaintances who were anxious to console her in her affliction.

Robin, before leaving for London, had arranged for one of Sir Hugh Derevale's granddaughters to stay with his twin as a companion and duenna. The present owner of Derevale Manor was only remotely connected with the old man who had once been designed as a husband for the young Annis Grenton. He was a kindly, pleasant man, now in middle-life with a wife and a grown-up family; he also gave house-room to various family dependants, and one of these was his cousin Emilia, who at over forty was unmarried and would have been in a sad way but for his benevolence.

At Derevale Manor, there was little for Emilia to do, and she was delighted to stay with Lucy at Pleasance. She was a vague, colourless woman who gave Lucy no trouble; her freedom was not curtailed by Emilia's presence, and it would have been easy to have met Stephen in the wood where she had so often met him. But that, as the parson's wife had seen them there – an unlucky chance since few people preferred to cut through the overgrown pathways for the sake of saving a few minutes – no longer seemed safe to Lucy.

Stephen had said in his letter that he would wait there each day at a given time. He did, but when a week passed and Lucy did not appear, he decided on boldness. His vanity was such that he could not believe she had discarded him; she had been too lost in love for him, too ready to fall in with any of his suggestions. Somebody, Stephen was sure, was keeping her away from him. He had not seen Emilia Henderson and imagined that she might be a formidable duenna.

It was no difficult matter to conceal himself in the grounds of Pleasance, and when all in the house had retired, he stood beneath Lucy's window which she had told him was at the front of the house with a balcony. Seeing the light of her candle he whistled softly a tune which was familiar to her, and which she would associate with him.

Almost instantly Lucy opened her window and stepped out upon the balcony. She leant over it, and made signs to him to go away, but that was Stephen's last intention, and although Lucy when locked into her bedroom had considered it an impossibility to escape by the window, he was bolder. There were footholes in the interstices of the rough stonework, and

Lucy watched with fascinated dismay as he climbed upwards and at length reached the balcony rail and stepped over it.

She protested, but Stephen only laughed, and as it was manifestly impossible to argue with him or to plead with him on her balcony where they might be overheard, there was nothing for it but to step back into her room, leaving him to follow.

All Lucy's instinct was now to be rid of the lover she had once adored, a fact of which he was soon made aware, for her body was rigid when he embraced it, and her lips unresponsive.

At first she tried to reason with him. Everything had changed. Her grandmother had found out about them, and it was partly the shock of this that had caused her death. Lucy had promised her as she lay dying that she would never marry Stephen. At that Stephen scoffed. Fondling Lucy, he assured her that such a promise given when she was in a distraught and remorseful state was not one by which she could be expected to abide, and when it dawned on him that she *wished* to abide by it, his love-making became more forceful.

Fearful of scandal, Lucy dared not raise an outcry, but she fought him as one possessed, wondering in a frenzied fashion how she could ever have imagined that she loved him, or have found that dark face now bent over her and alight with cruel laughter, anything but horrible. His hands were hard, he smelt of sweat and liquor. In the revulsion that swept over her there was positive loathing.

The struggle was fierce, for Lucy in spite of her slenderness possessed a wiry strength; nevertheless she would have been overcome finally had it not been for the highly polished parquet flooring. Stephen slid upon it, and fell. His head crashed on a corner of the great stone fireplace, and he lay motionless.

In horror, Lucy bent over him. She believed that for the second time in a few weeks she was in the presence of death, and instantly her thoughts turned to self-preservation. If Stephen, dead or alive, were to be found there in her bedchamber, her reputation would be irredeemably tarnished. Nobody would believe that a man she had not encouraged had climbed up to her room, and had forced himself upon her.

When the scandal broke, Mistress Foster would probably talk and so would old Susan.

But what could she do? She was not strong enough to haul Stephen to the balcony and to hoist his inert body over the rails. Even had she been it would have availed her nothing, for when his corpse was found the next day beneath her window it would be equally perilous to her.

It was then that she remembered the secret room behind the panelling. It would not be impossible to drag the body within and to leave it there.

Shudderingly, she decided that it was the only thing to do. Stephen's disappearance, she thought, would not cause any particular surprise as he had come and gone so frequently, and the only person likely to be much concerned was old Susan, who could not possibly connect Lucy with it.

The panel was slid aside. Stifling her revulsion, Lucy put her hands beneath Stephen's armpits and hauled him towards the aperture. She had contrived to get him half within the little room when his shoulders moved and he raised his head, whereupon Lucy with a stifled cry let him drop with a thud, and herself collapsed.

She did not wholly lose consciousness but minutes passed before she realized that she had been laid on her bed, and that Stephen was sitting in a chair at the foot of it. She raised herself on her elbow and stared at him. 'I thought you were dead,' she said.

Stephen, who was gingerly feeling a swelling lump on his forehead, but otherwise seemed little the worse, actually grinned at her : 'Belike I should have been if I hadn't come round in time. A man could be smothered in that cupboard, and if it were an unconscious man he might never arouse to make a clamour and get out alive.'

'You wouldn't have smothered,' said Lucy coldly. 'There is air enough, and it isn't a cupboard, but a secret chamber constructed years and years ago in case of need.'

'Why were you set on putting me in there?' he asked curiously.

'I've told you. I thought you were dead. None of this that has happened was of my seeking, but who would have believed me if they had found you here? It might not even be believed that I had nothing to do with killing you – that you slipped – that it wasn't . . .'

Her lips trembled and her eyes filled with tears. Stephen said with rough kindliness: 'Now don't start that, just when I was telling myself you were one in a million; not a silly little goose to cuddle and get the better of, but a girl with a man's spirit, who could fight with the best of 'em, and then without turning a hair, finish a chap off, and make a clean job of it.'

'I didn't finish you off. I didn't touch you.'

'No, but you'd got the nerve to look to the future. Tell me now, would you have gone on using this room, sleeping in it with a dead man behind the panel?'

'I – I suppose so. What else could I have done?'

Stephen threw back his head and laughed: 'You're a good plucked one. My old mam said once that for all your soft looks there was a hard streak in you, and that's God's truth.'

Lucy's eyes were round with wonder. Stephen's attitude was extraordinary. Once he had loved her; but she was sure that that love was now as dead as was hers for him; but at the same time he seemed to like her much better than when they had met as secret lovers. He wouldn't molest her again; she was sure of that, and there was respect in his gaze. The oddest thing was that she found herself reluctantly liking him. They met on equal ground as past antagonists, neither of whom had given way.

'I'm glad you're not badly hurt,' she said, and he shrugged and replied: 'I shall have a sore head tomorrow, but it won't be the first time. Let's have a look now at the grave you'd planned for me.'

'Only if you *were* really dead,' she protested.

He got up to peer round the opening in the panel and then walked into the little room. Lucy thought of the hidden paper and held her breath, but Stephen examined nothing, only remarked that as she had said there was air enough coming down the chimney-piece.

'It's a priest's hole,' he said. 'I've heard tell of such places, where those could shelter who were in flight after King Hal closed down the monasteries.'

Lucy, who knew that the secret room had been constructed

99

at a much later date, did not contradict him. He came back to her and said: 'I've done you no harm, Lucy, though I'd a mind to do harm tonight, seeing as I'd already lost you through no fault of mine. I wanted you then, and I could want you the more for the pluck of you; but you're not for me; maybe you're not for any man. It's this place, Pleasance, that's got the hold on you, though it can never be yours. You'll be aunt to your brother's brood, and live on here without a man.'

'It will still be my home,' Lucy said.

Stephen shrugged acquiescently: 'And you'd rather have that than make a new home for yourself with a man who'd love you? 'Tis a pity, for you'd bear fine sons. Make no mistake, my wench, it's not you and yourn that own Pleasance, but Pleasance that owns you. It'll be here long after you are dead and gone, and there'll be many sacrificed to it before it's no more than a ruin.'

'What matter if the sacrifices have been willing ones?' Lucy demanded.

Stephen gazed at her with some wonder. Standing there with her head thrown back, relieved that he was not dead and that she no longer wanted him, her expression was one of exaltation. A priestess dedicated to some secret cult might have looked much as Lucy looked now.

'Well, if that's what you want,' he said uncertainly, 'I'll make a pact with you. If there's aught I can ever do for you or yours then you let me know, and if you can do aught for me, I'll call upon you.'

'What can we do for each other except to part in friendship?'

'How would I know? It was a thought that came to me, a doubt that this was the end.'

'You won't even be staying in these parts,' said Lucy. 'You told me time and time again it was I who kept you here.'

'That's true. There's the world to be seen, and maybe a fortune to be made far from here. Even without that I'd not stay for long, not for all my mam's pleading. Maybe 'tis better the way things have turned out. Belike I'd have made a poor bailiff, even married to you, and with children and a fine home.'

'It was a summer madness that came upon us,' said Lucy, and even though she now felt so strong and sure there was regret for the enchanted, foolish girl she had been.

Stephen put out his hand, and after a slight hesitation Lucy gave him hers. Holding it, he said : 'I'd be the more content if I had your promise.'

'Very well then, I promise, if it means so much to you.'

She had a momentary fear that he might draw her to him and kiss her, but Stephen dropped her hand and turned to the window. He opened it and stood on the balcony, looking downward. 'It'll be a harder thing,' he said, 'to climb down than it was to climb up when I could see footholes above me, and it 'ud be risky for you to let me out through the house and a side door. There may be some here who sleep light. Sheets from your bed would serve as a rope.'

Lucy watched him in silence as he stripped her bed of its linen, twisted the sheets and knotted them together; then secured one end to the balcony, and clutching this improvised rope, let himself down towards the ground. The drop then was only a few feet, and standing beneath he waved an arm to her, and a minute later was on his way. Lucy pulled up the two sheets, unknotted them, smoothed out the creases as well as she could, and re-made her bed. She slid the panel across the secret spring which closed it.

Looking round, it seemed impossible that so much had happened within an hour, for all now was undisturbed. She was caught up in a mood of transcendent peace. Her future was secure, and she had nothing of which to be afraid.

✳ CHAPTER 15 ✳

Six months later Robin secretly married Aurora Fernand and the Queen's wrath subsequently fell upon him. Now that she had aged, Elizabeth had scant sympathy with love affairs, especially when they involved those who were attached to her person. She was more than ordinarily fond of the orphaned Aurora, and had promised that in due course she would select a husband for her, much to Aurora's misgiving, for she well knew that the Queen's choice would not fall on Robin, though he, too, was in her favour. If match there was to be for Aurora, it would be with one of the great nobles, not with a boy who was little older than herself, and who owned only a relatively small estate.

Because Robin's position at Court was a sinecure, it now irked him, though several others similarly placed were content, and there were those who envied him, more especially when the Queen decided to invest him with his great-grandfather's title. It was her fancy to have titled young men about her, and Robin because of his musical and poetic gifts was often in attendance.

Lucy, when she heard of the ceremony which had taken place at the Palace of Westminster, was elated, though aggrieved that she had not been present. Robin had hinted more than once that his twin would be honoured by a command to present herself at Court, but the Queen ignored this. Robin was so attached to his sister that she would deflect his attention to herself, whereas the Queen was becoming more and more insistent that she alone was to be the one object of interest.

Robin, now known as Sir Robert Grenton, had his detractors, and when by devious sources the secret of his marriage reached the ears of a courtier who was jealous of him, it was only a matter of time before the Queen was told of it.

A burst of fury was the result. The Queen, having discovered that the story was true, sent Aurora to Hunsdon with a chaperon who was bidden not to let her out of her sight. Robin was told ragingly that he had done that which imperilled his life. It was an act of high treason to wed one of the Queen's maids without her consent. They were both under-age, and Aurora was her ward.

Robin endeavoured to take all the blame for the wedding, but he was very young and was aghast at the Queen's wrath. She had always treated him with a playful affection, and although the great Earl of Leicester, had he been alive, could have told him that he too was terrified when he married unknown to the Queen, Robin was ashamed of the chilling dread which submerged him.

Later that day he was escorted to the Tower as a prisoner, not knowing if his life was forfeit, and there he remained for some weeks unaware that the Queen, who even in her anger had been touched by his pale face and ill-concealed fear, was gradually reconciling herself to the marriage.

Unknown to Robin, he had an advocate in the young Earl of Essex, who had always been friendly to him, and in whose praise Robin had written a much-admired sonnet. Now Essex did his best to soften the Queen. She was, he said, bringing out her cannon to mow down two sparrows, or rather a sparrow and a lark, for the little Aurora was no beauty, and would it not be a thousand pities to destroy a pleasing song-bird because of her? Robin was no fortune-hunter, said Essex, and in no great need of an heiress bride. There was nothing covetous about that poetic boy. As for Aurora, she had always been a misfit at Court. She was not only insignificant in appearance, but had no particular charm or cleverness. It was fortunate for her to have found a reputable young man as a husband.

Although Robin would not have agreed with Essex's assessment of Aurora, he would have been less desperately worried had he known that he was interceding for him; so would Lucy who was aghast when she heard of her brother's plight. In desperation she resolved to write personally to the Queen. She would have travelled to London had she thought that there was even a slight hope that the Queen would receive her; but she had no influence with anyone there, and the Queen had never shown any interest in her.

A letter, sent by a special messenger to Hampton Court Palace where the Court was now in residence, was almost certain to be received by the Queen and read. Lucy knew Elizabeth boasted that the humblest of her subjects would receive attention and justice if they appealed to her for such, and Lucy, though not humble, could assume humility in such a cause.

After many discarded attempts, her letter when finally composed was a masterpiece of tact and subtle flattery. Lucy wrote that she had had no suspicion of what Robin planned, or she would have spared no effort to dissuade him. She could not deny that he had behaved with ingratitude; so had

Aurora, though if the Queen would forgive the girl she promised to love her as a dear sister, knowing that whatever the Queen's cause for anger that would be her wish, if she pardoned a maid of whom she had been so tender.

As for herself, wrote Lucy, it was her grief that she had never had the opportunity to render the Queen the slightest service, though from her earliest childhood she had been taught to love her with an especially reverent love. But might she dare to humbly remind the Queen of her grandmother, Annis Grenton, who when a young girl had rendered some slight service to Queen Jane of blessed memory?

Queen Jane had believed that she drew strength from Annis Grenton, who had so loved her that she would gladly have given her life that she might live, had that been possible. His Majesty, King Henry had recognized this, for although Annis had not been one of the Queen's ladies, she had received one of the brooches which had been the King's especial gift to them. That brooch Lucy now enclosed with her letter, hoping it might serve to remind the Queen of the devoted loyalty of the Grenton family.

Reading through the letter, Lucy could think of nothing more to say, and hoped she had not said too much. It was, she admitted, not an entirely sincere letter, but it must have been many years since anyone had dared to be sincere with the great Queen. Flattery was her daily diet, the flattery which insisted that now in her old age she still had the appearance of a beautiful young girl, and that every one of her courtiers was hopelessly in love with her.

Lucy had tried to convey in her letter that although Robin was in debt to the Queen his family also had a claim on her gratitude, which claim might be met by forgiveness.

It was. A few days later Aurora was told to leave Hunsdon, and Robin was released from the Tower. The Queen then commanded them both to appear before her, and as the young husband and wife knelt at her feet she delivered judgement.

They were forgiven, but they were banished. Without spending another night at the palace they would start upon their journey to Pleasance. It would be long, the Queen said coldly, before she would wish to see either of them again; but they were still dear to her, and she would not revoke the title which she had seen fit to bestow upon Robin, and, since she believed them to be penitent she would not deny them her blessing. Robin would be required to answer for it to her if he did not make Aurora a kind husband.

Not willing to reveal that the Earl of Essex's plea for clemency had influenced her, she told Robin that he could be grateful to his sister who had pleaded for him and had reminded her of his family's constant loyalty. She took the brooch which Lucy had sent with her letter, and gave it to Robin, bidding him to return it to her. She removed a glittering bracelet from one of the many which slid up and down on her thin arm and fastened it upon Aurora's wrist.

Aurora, who truly loved the Queen, gazed up at her through a cascade of tears; Robin, who had never managed to love her, though he recognized her greatness, stammered out words of gratitude and remorse.

They dared not show any joy at being reunited until they were on their way to Pleasance, and then behind the drawn carriage curtains, Robin took his bride in his arms, and covered her small white face with passionate kisses.

It was true that Aurora was not precisely beautiful but Lucy, when she first saw her, thought she possessed a subtle quality which was greater than beauty. Robin had said that Aurora was 'different', and so she was. At eighteen she looked even younger. She was small, and her figure was scarcely more formed than a child's. She had a little pale face which was heart-shaped; she had red-gold curls and eyes of an almost golden hue; enormous eyes shaded by golden lashes. Those eyes, when lifted to meet Lucy's, struck upon her heart for they were not only beautiful in themselves but in their expression, which was one of loving kindness.

Much though Lucy had worried about Robin and the Queen's displeasure, she had also given a thought to the fact that his marriage automatically dispossessed her. She was no longer of importance as the mistress of Pleasance, but now she knew that was of no consequence. It was impossible that she and her sister-in-law could ever be rivals, or that Lucy could be made to feel unwanted.

Indeed within a few days Aurora said anxiously that she

feared it was selfish of her to be glad Lucy was not yet affianced. She supposed she would have to resign herself to that eventually, but she would certainly grieve and so would Robin when Lucy went away from Pleasance.

'I have no wish to wed,' said Lucy. 'I never shall have such a wish.'

Aurora looked at her doubtingly: 'You cannot be sure of that. You are only a few years older than I, and it is natural for a girl to hope for a husband and children; in most cases too for a home of her own, though I know that is not so with you. But although you love Pleasance dearly, you may not always put it first.'

'Do I put it first?' Lucy wondered. 'There is Robin, my twin, and twins as a rule are closer than an ordinary brother and sister . . . also I now have you to love.'

'We do not matter as much as the house. I wish I could think otherwise. To me it seems wrong. Pleasance has already been given too much.'

'But it is not unusual to love a family home. My grandmother felt as I did. She once said that Pleasance was the core of her heart, that she would not swear it was not part of her soul.'

'Poor woman,' Aurora commented gently.

'But don't you think it's worth loving?' Lucy persisted. 'You have seen it all now. All the rooms – the gardens, the dairy, the paddock and the horses. Are you not pleased with your new home?'

'It is a charming house,' said Aurora evasively, and then as Lucy looked disappointed she added: 'I feel differently from you. Because I love Robin dearly, I could live anywhere with him and be happy. It is the same with him. People who are made by God are more important than a house which has been built by man.'

'Are you very religious?' Lucy asked with some disquiet.

Humour flickered in Aurora's golden eyes as she shook her head: 'I have never considered myself such, but if I ever become so, I shall not make a religion of Pleasance. I think, Lucy, that it has been that – to others beside yourself. You have told me of your grandmother, and perhaps it was the same with those who lived here before her. I feel that suffering and wrong has been caused by such devotion, and the suffering still lingers.'

'How can you say such a thing?' Lucy tingled with indignation. She and Aurora had been walking through the gardens, and now they were resting on the stone seat on the terrace. Stone steps led down to the velvet-green lawns, shaded by cedar trees; beyond were the rose garden and the yew garden; buds were opening beneath the rays of the sun. All was peace and beauty and quiet content.

Aurora said: 'Robin tells me that your father felt much the same. He escaped from Pleasance and never wanted to return.'

'That was because he loved the life of the stage, and because he quarrelled with Grandmother when he fell in love with our mother.'

'Your grandmother thought she was not good enough for Pleasance. How fortunate she was, for in her marriage and love she had freedom. Your father offered up no sacrifices to Pleasance, though your grandmother did. Robin has told me about it.'

'What *could* he have told you?' Lucy enquired with secret apprehension.

'Much about their happiness with each other, not much about the estate,' Aurora said tranquilly. 'He has not loved it or studied it as you have; but he did tell me that his grandfather was unhappy here, though he endured it to please your grandmother. Had he loved her less he would have borne her away to London, but he felt, I suppose, that that would cause her too great a grief. She might have kept him with her longer; he might have lived to be as old as she was if they had lived elsewhere. Once she told Robin so.'

'She never said anything as definite as that to me, Aurora. I know she loved my grandfather intensely. She loved me the more because I have a likeness to him.'

'And because you feel about Pleasance as she did. Robin intends to give sufficient time to it as a landlord for the good of those whose living depends on it, but he will not allow the place to monopolize his entire life. He has always wanted to travel. My family live in France, and I hope to see much of them. It was sad to part when my father ordered me to come to England. Robin says that next year in the spring we will go there together. You could come with us. I thought of it when we made our plans, but I realize now that you would rather be here.'

Lucy said: 'One of the family should remain if you are planning a long visit to your French relations. No family estate can afford to be neglected.'

'Would it be as you have a land steward and his assistant, both competent, Robin says?'

'It is not the same thing. Grandmother, once she was in possession, never left Pleasance.' And then reluctantly, Lucy said: 'I believe the Lady Grenton who was her stepmother had a similar devotion. My great-grandfather neglected the estate, but she pulled it together. She was an heiress, and her fortune was spent on it.'

'And yet it was none of hers,' said Aurora wonderingly. 'She was childless and could not have inherited. Oh Lucy, can't you see that it is a monster; that it has already devoured too many lives?'

Stephen Reynolds had said much the same thing, Lucy remembered; but he was not a Grenton, and therefore could not be expected to understand. It did seem though as if those who married into the family were resentful. There was her grandfather who had lived here and taken the name of Grenton and now there was Aurora who, instead of pride and admiration, felt nothing but distaste.

'Do not have any regret for me, sister,' Lucy said. 'An absentee landlord is a bad thing for any family property; not that I have any real fear of that where Robin is concerned for since boyhood he has, as you say, always recognized his duty; but as we are fortunate in Reresby and his nephew whom he is training, and as I am qualified to manage the domestic side of the establishment, he can stay away for months at a time with a clear conscience.'

Aurora sighed. One could not be irritated by the pity in her eyes, thought Lucy, for it was such a tender pity.

'I am not convinced that my conscience will be untroubled,' said Aurora. 'Oh Lucy, we should insist on taking you with us. My uncle and aunt are well thought of at the French Court. There is such gaiety there, and also learning and culture. Paris is most beautiful. I have a cousin Raoul, who is some years older than you, who in his letters to me constantly says that when he marries he will seek an English bride. He is charming and handsome. Would you care to see his picture? I have a miniature of him.'

Lucy laughed. It was amusing to see her childish sister-in-law in the role of matchmaker. She said : 'Certainly, if you wish to show it to me; but even if I did marry it would not be to one of a different race.'

As insular as most of her class and sex, she thought of all Frenchmen as 'frogs', and was in full sympathy with Queen Elizabeth who years ago had refused to commit herself in marriage to a foreigner.

A new happiness had come to Lucy, for she realized now that Robin's marriage would make little, if any, difference to her. Aurora, sweet and loving though she was, would do battle with what she thought of as an obsession, and for many years, perhaps for ever, it would be she – Lucy – who was the real mistress of Pleasance.

PART THREE
1624-1646

❋ CHAPTER 16 ❋

When in the year 1624, Lucy Grenton held a year-old girl-child in her arms, and looked down into that small face with its formless features, there was a mist of tears before her eyes, and the knowledge that she gazed at one who was now heir to all that she had husbanded for more than three decades.

As mistress of Pleasance, Lucy had never been other than mistress in name, but this mite who had escaped death by a near miracle was the only child of Robin's only son.

Death had taken its toll during the last thirty years, and it often seemed strange to Lucy that she survived when so many had gone.

After a few months of marriage Robin and Aurora had left, as planned, on a visit to France, but with time France had become their permanent home and they only visited Pleasance, partly because as a source of revenue it demanded perfunctory attention, and partly for the sake of seeing Lucy. They had had three children, two daughters who married Frenchmen and now lived in Paris, and a son who married a French girl.

He had been the youngest of the family.

Robin and Aurora, who loved each other dearly and whose marriage was idyllically happy, had both died when in their early forties. Lucian, their son, fittingly named after his great-great-grandfather, had married soon afterwards. Lucy had only occasionally seen him when as a boy he had been brought over to England by his parents on a visit, and she had been overjoyed when two years after his marriage he had written to her to say that it was his plan to return to England and to live there permanently.

Because Lucy loved Pleasance so dearly, it had become a

grief to her that its rightful owners loved it so little. This took precedence over the satisfaction of being in possession. She had always insisted that she was no more than her twin's steward. For his part, Robin had been no grasping or profligate owner. He had derived a substantial income from his rent-roll, but was punctilious in exacting no more than the estate could afford to pay. Married to a wealthy wife who infinitely preferred her mother's country to England, his plan was that Pleasance should be nursed for his son, the heir, who might possibly prefer to live in the home of his father.

Lucy had little hope of it. The boy had been brought up as a Frenchman, and probably thought of France as his own country. More especially since Robin's death, her heart had been sore as she roamed from one nobly proportioned room to another, visited the stables, or walked in the perfect gardens.

No expense had been spared on the upkeep of Pleasance. The horse-breeding industry had developed over the years; the dairy had expanded to such an extent that it was a source of thriving prosperity. For all this Lucy was primarily responsible. She, who had been a poor hand at figures as a girl, had laboriously and with the aid of the head land steward taught herself to understand the intricacies of book-keeping and much else that would never be less than tedious to her. It was not enough that Robin, who found this simple, conferred with the land steward on his periodic visits, and saw all was in order. Lucy, herself, wanted to understand the mysteries of profit and loss in order that she could personally report to him.

Always there had been the hope that one day her beloved Pleasance would represent more to Robin than a source of income; a duty, and an inheritance to be passed down to his son and heir. To her it seemed incredible that he should have so little personal feeling for his ancestral home.

That he had not, was partly Aurora's fault, but who could blame Aurora who from the beginning so honestly stated her point of view? In any case, thought Lucy, it would have carried little weight with Robin, had he ever had any deep love for his home.

When he died, she was prepared for changes. It would be possible, she supposed, for Lucian to break the entail and to sell the estate. That might also break her heart, but how could

Lucian, of whom she knew so little, be expected to understand it or to pay much heed to it if he did understand?

His letter telling her that he and his wife, Marguerite, were sailing from France with their infant daughter had taken her completely by surprise, and her happiness was unflawed, for Lucian, wording his letter most affectionately, told her she must not for a moment suppose that there was any thought of dispossessing her. His memories of her were tender ones, and Pleasance would always be her home. His Marguerite was longing to meet her and he knew they would love each other.

Lucy had awaited their arrival with impatience. For the first time in years, she was really yearning for those of her own kin. And then when she was daily expecting them, fate had struck a mortal blow. In the stormy seas between Dieppe and Dover, the ship in which Lucian with his wife and child were sailing had sunk, and there were few survivors.

At first Lucy was told that all three of them were lost, but later she was informed that the baby girl was being cared for at Dover. Providentially, there were those amongst the survivors who had been acquainted with Lucian and Marguerite Grenton, and who knew of their destination. Therefore, the child had been easily identified.

Reresby, the land-agent who had grown grey in his service to the Grenton family, implored the grief-stricken Lucy to leave all to him; and he and his wife who was much his junior and well able to undertake the journey even in wintry weather, travelled to Dover to collect the baby girl.

So here was Lucy, approaching her fifty-first birthday, and at this mature age virtually a mother. It was true that in France the baby had married aunts and several young cousins, but since her inheritance was in England, and as Lucian had announced that he intended his child to be reared in the home of her forefathers, Lucy was satisfied that she would be claimed only for occasional visits to her French kinsfolk.

The baby was asleep when she was first put into Lucy's arms, who cuddled her to her breast and murmured loving words. The babe was the precious salvage of disaster, and it would be no fault of Lucy's if she did not grow up to be strong and beautiful and devoted to Pleasance. That, after all, was what the child's parents had planned, and one could forget that Aurora would have deplored it.

'She is going to be her great-great-grandmother over again,' Lucy told the grey-haired Reresby, who was one of the few left on the estate to remember Annis.

It was true that the babe had the same faintly golden skin, the same brilliant blue eyes. She was a strong infant, with round, firm limbs and curling fair hair. Even her name had some faint resemblance to Annis, for she had been christened Andrea.

'I shall need to be so wise and firm and loving,' Lucy told the land-agent, who benevolently watched her as she fondled the child.

It was as though with the little Andrea's arrival not only Lucy, but the old house itself, was bestirred to a new life. Pleasance once more took that which was its right, the devotion of an owner.

A so-called owner, Stephen Reynolds would have said, reflected Lucy with a smile, and thought that one day it might be quite interesting to have a talk with Stephen, who oddly enough after an absence of several years was living only a few miles away.

Nobody had any precise knowledge of what had happened to him during the years in which none had heard of him, and he had been forgotten.

He had re-appeared some seven or eight years ago as an entirely different character; married and with young children. A middle-aged man of sober countenance, with money at his command. To the astonishment of all, and to the indignation of those who remembered his humble origin and his far from reputable history, he had purchased the tumbled-down manor house and the neglected land that had belonged to Sir Hugh Derevale, whose descendants had long since scattered.

Nobody knew how Stephen had made his fortune as he undoubtedly had, but many a guess was hazarded. It was known that he had been one of Drake's men, but Drake had died years before. When people spoke of Stephen Reynolds they were wont to whisper the word 'piracy'. Lucy would not have been surprised to know for certain that this was the source of her old lover's wealth. He had been bold and ruthless enough, sufficiently lawless to sail the high seas beneath the skull and crossbones, lucky enough to escape the violent end which generally overtook such rogues, and to garner an ill-gotten fortune.

In any case he had settled down and that, perhaps, was not too surprising, for even in the days when Lucy had known and loved him, he had had some such inclination. It would have happened that way had his mother succeeded in forcing Annis Grenton to permit their marriage.

Lucy, who had long ago dismissed Stephen from her thoughts, reflected on the strangeness of that past infatuation. It seemed beyond belief that she could once have longed to be Stephen's wife; had asked for nothing better than to be given the old Dower House as their home, and to rear his children, while he took up the duties of land steward at Pleasance. She wondered if in that case her twin would have made his home in France. Probably not, for had their grandmother lived, she would not have tolerated such absenteeism. Aurora, for all her gentle obstinacy, would have been forced to give way to her, though Lucy, naturally, had been unable to coerce either of them.

There could have been a happier destiny for them all, reflected Lucy, even though Robin and Aurora had been so devoted. Their children would have been reared at Pleasance, and if Lucy had had a family they would all have played together as cousins. Certainly her position would have been a subordinate one, but would that have irked her? She would still have been part of Pleasance.

However, when she occasionally saw Stephen it was difficult to believe that he had any connection with the man she had once loved. He had become so respectable, she thought with amusement. His wife, who was a native of Edinburgh, was a dowdy, small woman, who could never have been remarkable for good looks, and their three children were very well-behaved. Lucy knew from hearsay that Stephen had done much with the neglected estate he had bought; the old house had been repaired, the land assiduously cultivated, and finally he had started up as a sheep farmer, with much profit to himself.

When he and Lucy met by chance, courteous salutations were exchanged, but they had no social contact. Stephen might be, and probably was, richer than any of the old families living in the district, but not one of them would have received him as an equal. Yet, later on, when little Andrea was between six and seven years old, Lucy, feeling that the child's life was too isolated and that she was in need of young companionship, sent her to the nearest dame's school in order that she should mix with other children, and here she met one of the Reynolds brood.

Although a servant took Andrea to school and brought her home when lesson time was over, she experienced some of the rough and tumble natural to the village children, and one day displayed a bruised cheek having set up a strong protest when an older girl had torn off her hair-ribbon and appropriated it.

'Debby hit me, but I hit her back,' announced Andrea proudly, 'and her nose bled, and then I fell down and a big boy picked me up, and went after Debby and made her give up my hair-ribbon.'

She held out the strip of blue silk, which was torn and useless now, and Lucy's heart misgave her. Fraternity with such children had its undesirable aspect.

'He was a very nice boy,' Andrea told Lucy. 'He said he would bring me home if I liked, instead of waiting for Hester; but I think that was really because he wants to see our horses. He's much bigger than me, and too old, he says, to be at such a school where there are more girls than boys.'

'You are also getting too old for it,' said Lucy. 'I shall have to make some other arrangement for you. It might be better for you to have a governess, and for the children at the parsonage to share lessons with you.'

Andrea, not particularly interested in plans for her future education, said coaxingly: 'May the boy see the stables and the horses, Aunt Lucy? I could tell him so, when I go to school tomorrow. He is three years older than me, and his name is Ben Reynolds. He was very kind and said he would always protect me while he was there, but he would like to see the horses, especially as I told him that three little ones had been born only last week.'

'Very well. You can tell him to come along after school, and then I can thank him for being good to you.'

The fight in which the child had been involved convinced

Lucy that she was wrong in thinking that while she was so young the company of the village children could do her no harm. The housekeeper who had been at Pleasance when Andrea was first brought there, had been against it from the start, saying that it was not seemly. She was right, probably, Lucy admitted, though to her mind it was absurd to apply social distinctions to children who were little more than babies.

As it chanced, she saw Ben Reynolds the next day when he was in the paddock, watching the beautiful horses who were being exercised. Andrea had escaped the maid in charge of her to tag after the boy who was plainly the object of her first hero worship. He was a tall, handsome lad who bore some resemblance to the young Stephen. He had the same thick, dark hair, olive skin and laughing eyes; but there was kindness in his laughter, and his mouth was sensitive.

As Lucy listened to the two children talking together, she thought Stephen had been luckier than he deserved to have such a son; and for all she knew his other children might be equally likeable.

Ben could ride, he told Andrea, who even at eight years old was a better horsewoman than her great-aunt had ever been; but there were, he said, only carthorses and one or, two old hacks at Derevale Manor. Lucy told him that as a reward for being kind to Andrea he could borrow a mount, and ride sometimes with her.

The boy thanked her in a mannerly fashion, but said he would soon be going away to school. His father had arranged for him to be tutored at Oxford by a master who received pupils in his own home. He had two older brothers already there.

'In the holidays then,' said Lucy kindly.

Within a month a governess had been engaged for Andrea, who henceforth kept her to a strict schedule of work and play. Occasionally, in the long summer vacation, Ben Reynolds would visit Pleasance and would ride with Andrea, with a groom in attendance. The child looked forward to these visits, which continued intermittently for years; but in the long months between them she seemed to forget Ben and rarely spoke of him. Nevertheless, one day when she was verging on thirteen, she came to Lucy in tears.

They might never see Ben again, she said dolefully. He had that morning been over to Pleasance to say goodbye. He had quarrelled with his father and had run away from home.

❋ CHAPTER 17 ❋

A day later, Stephen Reynolds called upon Lucy, and without preamble told her that if she had any idea of his son's whereabouts he expected her to be candid with him. Lucy received him coolly, explaining that she had not seen Ben for some months, and never had seen much of him, though she had given orders that a horse was to be saddled for him, and that he was to be allowed on request to share her niece's hour for riding.

Now she regretted that she had allowed that companionship, for she certainly did not wish to be involved in the boy's troubles with his family. Andrea was unhappy because she would no longer see the admired Ben, though Lucy was inclined to welcome that as the boy was on the verge of manhood.

'He's always been the stone egg in the nest,' Stephen grumbled. 'His brothers are all for the land, and I'd a mind to buy more, to portion it out equally to them to be responsible for, and to become their own when it pleases the Good Lord to take me. Fine, honest lads they are, the pair of them, but not Ben. Our cross, so my wife says. The Lord's hand has been laid heavily upon us.'

Lucy stared at him in amazement. Could it be Stephen, rumoured to have amassed wealth by no orthodox means, who was now so sanctimonious? She thought that meeting her gaze his weather-beaten face reddened slightly. He evidently felt that some explanation was called for, and said: 'I've long since repented of my heathenish ways, and my wife was always a God-fearing woman: a Scot she is, and proud to be a member of a fine family. Mayhap you've heard of John Knox?'

'The preacher? Yes, certainly. He was a famous figure in his day. Is your wife one of his descendants?'

'She is, and she never forgets it.'

'Then no doubt she made a convert of you when she married you.'

'She did.'

Lucy was amused and slightly mocking. 'In which case it's not surprising if you are now ardent for Presbyterianism. I have always heard that a sinner is the best material for piety.'

'Well, that's what the Good Book tells us, isn't it, Lucy?' Stephen spoke with a simplicity which against her will, Lucy found disarming. 'There's the parable of the Prodigal Son and the Good Lord's forgiveness of publicans and sinners. My boys and girls with such a mother as I've given them, won't have the excuse for wildness that I did, but Ben has stood out against me from the time he was first able to read and write. Yawning and falling asleep at family prayers; laughing and making game of his brothers when they tried to show him the error of his ways; taking a beating without blubbering. He's run off more than once and been brought back again, and now he's been gone for a day and a night although I've sent my men to search for him: knowing your little maid had a fondness for him, I did think he might have come to you with his troubles, and have got on your soft side.'

Lucy admitted that Andrea had told her Ben was in trouble at home, and was determined to cut adrift, though Lucy had known nothing about it until after he had gone. She would not have sheltered him, a boy of that age, she assured Stephen, without letting his parents know it. What was the particular trouble that had caused the last act of rebellion?

'Bless me if I can put a name to it,' said Stephen. 'It's what the boy has the impudence to call my hypocrisy. Religion — our way of religion — is tedious, he says. Can't stomach it, he told his mother. He's all for the Church and the Bishops and the King, who's bringing such a mort of trouble on the country. At Oxford where I sent him to be tutored, he made a friendship with one Philip Buxton who comes from round Hereford way. A gentleman's son, he is, who'll be an army officer in a year or so, and has done nothing but spur Ben on to join up with him.'

'Perhaps he's with this Philip Buxton now,' Lucy suggested. 'That boy's family might be sympathetic to him.'

Stephen's face darkened. 'I'd thought of it myself,' he said, 'but if he's thrown himself upon that lot, he can keep away from me and the rest of the family. I won't raise a finger for him.'

What had he got against the Buxtons, Lucy wanted to know, and was genuinely curious. After all there were several families of ancient lineage still living in the district, and Stephen, she presumed, was not on antagonistic terms with all of them. But his lips curled with an unpleasant scorn when Lucy spoke of those who were her friends.

'Those old families are dying out,' he said. 'They've not kept themselves in the swim as you have at Pleasance, with the horse trade and the farming and dairy. That 'ud be beneath the most of them. It's the merchant class that is buying up the country estates, and there's few of them as are Episcopalians. There's those who sneer at us and call us Puritans, but mark my word, Lucy, before long it'll be at your peril if you own to being anything else.'

'Not a pleasant prospect,' said Lucy lightly. 'One had thought that the days of religious intolerance were over. The great Queen was lenient over such difference in outlooks, and even King James was reasonable, except over the matter of witches. We cannot all see eye to eye, Stephen, though it's much pleasanter if members of a family agree about important matters. I think you should, without rancour, allow your son to hold his own opinion. It is not a crime to be loyal to one's King.'

'Mayhap it will be within a few years or less,' retorted Stephen. 'Haven't you thought it out for yourself, Lucy? The taxing alone is enough to rile any man of spirit. A shipping tax for those who live inland – well, I ask you – and who can be loyal to a King who knows nothing of loyalty to his subjects? What mountebank is this who calls himself divine, and acts the tyrant by dismissing Parliament and imposing his own rules?'

Lucy, who now that she had recovered from her first astonishment over Stephen's conversion to a faith which she would never have expected to appeal to such a buccaneer, was becoming bored. She stifled a yawn, and as a sign that it was time he took his departure, rose from her chair.

'I have never had an inclination towards politics,' she said. 'Not many women have; but my allegiance is to my King, whatsoever his faults or mistakes. I am sorry I cannot help you with any information about your son, who has always struck me as being an agreeable lad. I suspect you are fonder of him than you imagine, and I hope you will make an effort to find out if he is safe with this friend of his. He is still very young; not yet sixteen. I might remind you though that if he does join the army it is only what you did yourself, years ago.'

'I was in a different case. There's no likeness between his and mine,' said Stephen angrily; and then his gaze softened as it rested on Lucy: 'When you and I first met, those were happy days,' he said.

'We thought they were,' conceded Lucy, who had never forgotten to thank the fate that had separated them.

'You were the prettiest thing, and as soft-eyed as a doe,' he remembered. 'I shall always remember the way we parted. You thought you'd killed me, and you'd have made that room behind the panel my grave.'

Lucy's anger flared: 'I certainly never thought I had killed you. It was nothing to do with me . . . you slipped . . . it was your fault for forcing yourself into my room.'

He shook his head reprovingly: 'You always were one to get into a quick rage, but it suits you. You look of a sudden ten years younger. We parted good friends, Lucy, and although I married Elspeth and have made her a good husband, I never forgot you, and the pact we made. You've not forgotten it either, have you?'

'That we would help each other if we were ever in need of help? No – I've not forgotten it, but I hope I've convinced you that I can't help you over your son. I can only advise you to try to find out where he is, and if he has gone to his friend's family to be tolerant, and to give him your blessing.'

'I'll never do it. He's near broken his mother's heart. When he was born we knew he'd be our last, seeing as Elspeth was gone forty, and was mortal bad bringing him into the world. Our Benjamin, we called him, and though there's been nothing but trouble with him, she's fixed on him, poor woman. She's wrestled with the devil for him. There's been no spoiling of any of them, and although Elspeth was never one to raise her hand to them, she beat Ben time and again until he got too strong for her and stood up to her. Then she handed him over to me, and I've had to take a whip to him – aye, even as I prayed over him.'

Lucy felt a strong surge of compassion for the luckless Ben. She said: 'How can you think that's the right way to bring up a boy and to make him love you?'

'It worked with his brothers,' Stephen retorted, 'though they didn't need the same beatings. A threat of it was enough to make them shake, but never Ben – he defied me to do my worst.'

'He must have more courage and spirit than his brothers, and you always admired spirit. It's my belief that he means more to you than the others. I don't suppose it's too late, even now. Why not show him that a father can be kind and understanding?'

'That'd be playing into the devil's hands,' said Stephen in sombre tones.

'If that's your outlook, there's nothing more I can say.'

When Stephen left, Lucy pondered over Ben, and hoped that the boy would not be forced to return to his family. Almost anyone could surely do better by him.

Some weeks passed, then Andrea received a letter, conveyed to her by one of the journeying pedlars who often undertook such commissions. It was from Ben and she took it to Lucy. They read it together.

Ben, as Lucy had surmised, was in Hereford with his friend Philip Buxton and his family. He was a good penman and quick at figures, therefore Philip's father had found work for him with the family attorney, though this wasn't an apprenticeship, Ben explained. Determined to become a soldier, and old enough to enlist in a year or so, he would not consent to bind himself, as would be required for an apprentice in any trade or profession.

The letter went on to explain that Philip was on friendly terms with Prince Rupert, the King's dashing and handsome cousin, who was of much the same age as himself. Prince Rupert appeared to be the type that any boy could hero worship. Adventure was life itself to him, as it was to Philip, wrote Ben, but although soldiering was to be his profession, he was also gifted at science and drawing.

'What is science, Aunt Lucy?' asked Andrea.

'Experiments,' Lucy answered vaguely.

'This Philip Buxton has promised to make Ben known to the Prince,' Andrea said, reading on. 'He'll never come back, will he? He's already made a place for himself with these people.'

Hereford was not so far away, said Lucy, and men, however adventurous, did tend to return to their home towns, though often only after the lapse of years.

'Ben asks me not to forget him, but with so much in his new life, it is he who will forget me.'

Andrea's voice was doleful, and although she was but thirteen, Lucy was aware of a fleeting relief because Ben Reynolds had been removed from her immediate orbit. They would soon forget each other.

Ben did not write again, and to Andrea his memory dimmed. She was growing into womanhood, and was accounted more than ordinarily handsome. Lucy was proud of her and worried about her. She, herself, was ageing, and for the last few years she had not been strong. Her doctor warned her that her heart was weak, and urged her to rest as much as possible. At seventeen, Andrea was capable and of a thoughtful disposition. Although she mingled in local society, and was aware of the admiration she evoked, she was not impressionable, and assured Lucy that it would be a long, long time before she wanted to marry; and although at her tender years this was not an avowal to be taken seriously, Lucy often wondered if she would be likely to meet anyone suitable to assume the name of Grenton, and to share the administration of the estate with her.

What a splendid thing, thought Lucy, if Andrea could be matched with one capable of a devoted love for Pleasance; more so than that which Andrea evinced. Her interests were wide, whereas devotion demanded concentration. Lucy wondered at her, for without any prompting Andrea had become an enthusiastic gardener. Also, without any particular encouragement she had developed a gift for painting.

Even as a child, this facility had been pronounced and a master in the art of painting had been engaged to give her lessons. From him, Andrea learnt how to paint on ivory; delicate little miniatures of flowers and birds and even tiny landscapes. She finally outvied her master, who admitted that she had nothing more to learn from him, and now, more ambitiously, she was painting in oils; not only garden scenes of Pleasance, which in Lucy's eyes were wonderfully beautiful, but portraits of anyone who could be induced to sit for her.

Lucy was a good subject, as she needed to rest frequently, and Andrea's drawing-book was full of sketches of her aunt, sometimes in pencil, sometimes in crayon. In her old age Lucy was still beautiful with her silver hair and olive skin, and her dark, wistfully tender eyes.

Sometimes it seemed to Lucy that the versatile Andrea was suffering a disadvantage through her quiet country life, and this view was echoed in the letters which were received from France. Andrea's two aunts had both produced large families, and although, while she was still a child, they had agreed that it was the right thing for her home to be at Pleasance, they now wrote suggesting that she should be permitted to pay them a long visit. Both lived on the outskirts of Paris, and their husbands held high positions at the French Court. Andrea, if she visited them, would be given every opportunity to meet the illustrious and might well make a brilliant alliance.

Such invitations had become the more pressing since Andrea, having executed a self-portrait miniature, had sent it to the girl cousin who most frequently corresponded with her. It was evident that not only her talent, but also her beauty had come as a surprise to her French relations, who had forthwith written to Lucy to say that such fair, English looks were much admired, and that it was important to give such a lovely young heiress a chance to spread her wings.

Andrea took this exhortation lightly. There was time enough; she was perfectly happy, and occupied from morning to night. The gardens were being re-constructed to a design of her own, and she planted many of the new flowers which had lately been introduced into England from Holland. That spring of 1641 there were groves of many-coloured tulips, and laburnum trees in a shower of golden rain. In addition, Andrea was also proficient at embroidery work; taught this by Lucy, and was capable at most household duties. The servants loved her and there was little she did not know about horses.

Lucy sometimes felt that she was Annis Grenton over again, but there was a subtle difference, for although Andrea closely resembled Annis in appearance, seemed indeed to be almost a replica of her portrait in the picture gallery, Annis had never possessed Andrea's detachment.

Andrea was fond of her home. At the present time she had no desire to leave it, but it would not, Lucy thought, break her heart if in the future she was fated to live elsewhere. It did not strike Andrea as tragic because, as the old families died out, their estates were bought by wealthy merchants; there had to be changes, she said, when Lucy spoke sadly about this. A new and less omnipotent aristocracy was springing up, and probably even kings and queens would find that their power was limited. Was it not because King Charles could not reconcile himself to this that there was now such a rift in the country? It was not alone the taxation he imposed, but that a great nation would not submit to being ruled by one man who believed he could not err.

It was a heartbreaking pity that the King saw himself in this light, said the seventeen-year-old Andrea. She agreed with Lucy that in any circumstances her allegiance was given to the King, but one could not blind oneself to his imperfections. He must have a weak character, thought Andrea. It seemed certain that he had given too much power to the Duke of Buckingham, and after his assassination to Queen Henrietta Maria.

Lucy observed dryly that Andrea's relations in France had nothing but pity for the Queen who was so unpopular in England, and that if her great-niece entertained such disloyal thoughts it was as well that there had been no opportunity of presenting her at Court as her Aunt Solange had urged.

At this reproof Andrea tried to explain that her loyalty was something of the spirit, not of the reason. She was not an 'accepting' person, that was why she would never be a really good churchwoman. She would want to argue with the Puritans as much as with the Catholics or the Episcopalians.

'You are a clever girl,' said Lucy, 'but it is happier for a woman not to be too clever.'

At least, thought Andrea, she was sufficiently clever to deceive her great-aunt. Lucy had no suspicion that although Andrea would be delighted to visit her relations in Paris, the project had been dismissed as an impossibility because of Lucy's health. Lucy was dearer than anything in the world; far dearer than Pleasance. Andrea, from her very soul, would have agreed with her grandmother Aurora who had said that people were more important than houses.

❋ CHAPTER 18 ❋

The year of 1641 saw the real start of the trouble which was to split the country asunder. Even Lucy who despised the Puritans had to admit that in this part of the world they were now predominant. The services at the parish church were but sparsely attended, but the chapels – ugly, recently built, and often with no more than tin roofs – were full to overcrowding.

There was no fear now, as there would have been in Elizabeth's day, of openly criticizing the monarch. Pamphlets were printed abusing Charles for his injustices; for the fact that he promoted bishops to occupy offices of State; receiving members of the Church in the Royal Closet, for the purpose of listening and acting on the advice which he refused to consider from those qualified to give it. His devotion to his Catholic French wife was another cause for criticism, for it was believed that Henrietta Maria's supreme aim was to suppress the Protestant religion; even such a variation of it as Charles's, which many considered not far removed from allegiance to Rome. Scandalous stories were circulated about the Queen. She was said to be a witch who had put a spell on her royal husband, instigating him in his worst follies, as when he had ordered the seizure of all private moneys in the Tower Mint where for years the City merchants had been accustomed to deposit their spare cash in safe custody, as they had supposed.

But nothing was safe from the King's grasping hands, and pictures of himself and his wife and children, laden with ill-gotten jewels, were distributed throughout the country.

There was already a full-scale rebellion in Scotland, and the sorely pressed Irish were soon to follow suit. Lucy, realizing that she and her kind were now in the minority, felt as though the whole world as she knew it was slipping away from her.

From France came alarmed letters. Why not leave England, Andrea's relations urged, while it was still possible to leave? Arrangements could be made for Andrea and for Lucy too to board a French ship. There were pages of closely written, anxious advice.

But Lucy would not consider leaving her country at this time of crisis, and Andrea who knew that Lucy's health was now so precarious that the journey would be dangerous, contrived to send a letter to France without her knowledge. In the letter she explained the impossibility of abandoning Lucy, and assured her French kinsfolk that so far as she could judge they were in no danger of molestation, even though their home was situated in the centre of a Puritan stronghold.

The owners of Pleasance had always been well respected, and who would be likely to harm two women whose very defencelessness was their best protection?

Lucy had no fear whatsoever, and if Andrea sometimes suspected that the now inevitable upheaval was bound, to change their whole way of life, she did not say so.

✳ CHAPTER 19 ✳

One could, with time, become accustomed to anything, even to Civil War. Lucy frequently made some such remark during years of stress and enforced seclusion.

Although none had personally molested them, their normal life had been disrupted. Early in the war, the horses, by the breeding and selling of which the estate had for generations been chiefly maintained, were seized and taken away by a company of Roundheads, who arrived to 'requisition' them. In those early days there was some show of order. The officers in charge of the company informed Lucy that she would be recompensed in due course, and gave her a signed paper to amplify the promise. One horse would be generously left for their personal use.

Lucy listened with silent scorn. Doubtless they would be recompensed, when the King returned to power – not by the Parliamentary troops.

After that, servants began to drift away from Pleasance. Most of them were in sympathy with the rebels, and the menfolk had sworn allegiance to their cause. Only a few of the oldest servants remained, and Andrea suspected that this was due less to loyalty than to the fact that they could not get employment elsewhere.

Lucy, old and frail, and in uncertain heath, was still dauntless. These bad times would pass, she insisted, and the King whom the rebels had deposed would soon be reinstated and in greater power than ever before. At first it seemed as though that might be, for in the early battles all the advantages fell to the King's party. The Prince Rupert of whom Ben Reynolds had written, was now an inspired leader, and at the Battle of Worcester Lucy and Andrea heard that he had scattered his opponents like chaff before the wind.

Lucy was prepared to bring out the treasured gold plate, only used for the most ceremonious occasions, and to have it melted down in order to swell the King's resources. Andrea agreed, but in the end this proposed sacrifice came to nothing, for they were not in touch with any of the Royalist headquarters where such valuables could be received.

Andrea finally dug unaided a trench in the yew garden, wrapped much of the gold and their most valuable jewels in cloth bags and tin cases, and buried them there, carefully planting shrubs over the earth she had disturbed.

The tide turned against the royal forces with the Battle of Marsden Moor and later that of Nazeby. News reached the two women at Pleasance that Archbishop Laud had been impeached by Parliament, condemned to death and finally beheaded.

Now there was fear of the King's ultimate fate, for Prince Rupert had been forced to surrender the citadel at Bristol which he had besieged and held for two years. When it was known that the King and his army were in full flight before the Parliamentary forces, there was rejoicing in the villages near Pleasance, though such rejoicing mainly took the form of additional psalm-singing. Until now the local Roundheads had treated the few remaining Royalist owners of large estates with surly indifference; but now after these crushing defeats, Lucy and Andrea heard of various lawless acts. Several churches and big houses were sacked, the latter beneath the eyes of their helpless owners, who were usually too old or too few to put up an effective resistance.

'We can hardly expect to escape the same treatment,' said Lucy, her lips trembling, though her head was raised in proud defiance. 'It is as well that we have various good hiding places for our gold and valuables. They are unlikely to be discovered.'

Andrea, for her part, was surprised that they had so far suffered little beyond isolation and evidences of dislike, which were hard to endure from those who had once been friendly. In the shops she was served unwillingly, the money she tendered accepted as though it were tainted. Even had they not been bereft of staff, which meant that the dairy was now closed, they could have supplied little produce for the market. Most of the livestock had been sold at the beginning of hostilities when it had still been possible to sell.

Lucy looked at Andrea with an aching heart. Her beautiful

girl was so strong and fearless, so constantly brave, but at twenty-one her careless youth was a thing of the past. Her gowns were shabby; she had not bought a new one for over three years, her hands were rough with housework and gardening; she was debarred from the slightest pleasures.

What would become of her? Lucy knew that her own health was increasingly precarious, and that even had it been possible to leave the country she would never have survived it. If only the kindly Dr Beale, who was one of the few old friends they still saw, had not told Andrea that her life hung upon a thread. Then it might have been arranged for her to escape from what was now almost a prison. But Andrea, as Lucy knew without telling, would never leave her.

Dr Beale, by virtue of his profession, moved freely between friend and foe, the latter availing themselves thanklessly of his services, the former eagerly welcoming him. It was from Dr Beale that the two lonely women at Pleasance heard the various details of the conflict which sometimes seemed as though it would be never ending.

'I have a message for you, Mistress Grenton,' the good doctor said one day. 'Stephen Reynolds of Derevale sends to tell you that he has done his utmost to fulfil his part of the pact. If you have had nothing to fear until now, it is because he has exerted his good offices on your behalf.'

It was long since Lucy had given Stephen a thought, and confined to the house as she was, she had not even seen him in passing.

'Years ago, he promised to serve me if he ever could,' she explained to Dr Beale. 'His mother was my grandmother's personal maid. Time changes all, as Andrea impresses on me. I suppose he is now a personage with those who declare themselves to be our lords and masters.'

Dr Beale assented with a shrug: 'It would seem so. Reynolds, at his age, has seen no fighting but he has opened his purse strings, so I hear, and two of his boys have from the first been under Cromwell's command. The younger was killed at Worcester; the elder is safe as far as is known.'

'Has anything been heard of the one who ran away from home before he was grown?' Andrea asked.

Lucy glanced at her in surprise, for this was the first time in years that Andrea had spoken of Ben. Dr Beale knew nothing of him, though he had been told before the outbreak of hostilities that he had thrown in his lot with a Royalist family of some distinction.

'I suppose we have fared better than most,' said Lucy, when she and Andrea were alone. 'Stephen Reynolds has a heart after all, and for me he had always a kindness. Although we are almost servantless and have lost so much in the way of stock, we have not been threatened or over-run. I wonder how Stephen has managed it.'

'He has probably spread it abroad that you are in secret sympathy with their cause,' Andrea said thoughtlessly, and then wished she had not spoken, for the colour rose in Lucy's thin cheeks and she nervously clenched her hands.

'If I believed he had done that, I should be forced to contradict it,' she said.

'Oh, Aunt Lucy, no! Does it matter what they think? Let us keep Pleasance if we can. Some day we may be able to open up all the rooms again, and buy horses to breed and thus to start afresh. Meanwhile, if we can stay here more or less forgotten, let us be thankful for it.'

Andrea's one great hope was that her great-aunt might be allowed to live out the remainder of her years in peace. If she were to be driven from the home which she so dearly loved, and which she had cherished throughout her long life, it would be a cruel end for her. There was no sacrifice Andrea would not have been willing to make to avoid that heartbreaking calamity.

'You are right,' Lucy agreed after reflection. 'Although the King's enemies may seem to have prevailed, it is only temporary. Pray God they may do His Majesty no harm; but even if anything so terrible should come about, he has sons, one of whom will in time come into his own again. Never doubt that, Andrea, for I am as sure of it as that the sun will rise and set tomorrow.'

Fugitives from the Royalist armies were known to be seeking refuge in the houses of those who espoused the King's cause, and placards were exhibited in even the smallest market town offering rewards for the apprehension of any Royalist, and threatening punishment to those who befriended one. Nobody knew the whereabouts of Prince Rupert, but there was a price set on his daring head, and it was said that should he fall into the hands of his enemies he would be hanged, if not drawn and quartered.

Andrea, doing her scanty shopping in the village, heard that the King had surrendered to the Scots, and that the garrison at Oxford had surrendered to the rebels. On her much-valued horse, Andrea rode home with a heavy heart. Lucy questioned her so earnestly that she found it impossible to keep the bad news from her, and for the first time Andrea saw her great-aunt completely broken down and weeping miserably.

'As soon as it is possible, you must leave here,' said Lucy later in the day. 'Why should there be any objection to your joining your mother's family in France?'

'Others have been stopped, Aunt Lucy. And what of you? What of Pleasance?'

Lucy's eyes were swimming with tears as she gazed out of the window upon the gardens she loved. They were neglected now, for although Andrea had done her best, it was impossible to keep them in order without several gardeners. Now there was only one old man, who hobbled groaningly along the paths, sweeping up the dead leaves, and occasionally pruning a straggling bush; but doing nothing for the once-velvet lawns where the grass grew tall, or for the yew hedges which had not been clipped for many months.

Nevertheless, old Joseph who had been in late middle-age when Andrea was a baby, and who in a grumpy, inarticulate way had adored her then and still did, was of great value and solace to both women. Nobody in the village gave a thought to the old man when he went on messages; nobody guessed that the occasional letters which were sent from France through a trusted source were finally passed secretly to Joseph. It was Joseph who plodded along to Dr Beale's house should he be wanted before his weekly visit was due; Joseph who bought from the shops as though for his own use goods which were begrudged to the owners of Pleasance, hated now as were all their kind.

'I am not likely to live much longer,' said Lucy, 'and we have friends here who would take me in were you gone. For a time Pleasance must be left. I do not believe it will be for ever. One day it will be given back to you and yours, though no doubt if we were not here it would be handed over to some rebel family. We must devise a way of getting a letter to France on your behalf. In Solange's last letter, she said that it would be possible to bribe the captain of a ship; a cargo ship which would make at least a pretence of unloading at Harwich while it awaited your arrival. Never fear but that the captain will contrive to get a message to us, bidding you make all speed to join him.'

Andrea said with surprise: 'I did not know Aunt Solange had written with such a plan in mind.'

'It was better not to tell you. I hoped to be able to persuade you to leave when the message arrived.'

'Aunt Lucy, I would not go without you. How would it benefit me? I should never know one moment's peace, wondering how you were faring.'

'As to that, it's of no great consequence what happens to an old woman; but if it would be of greater ease to you, I am prepared to venture with you,' said Lucy tranquilly. 'Mayhap I should live to weather the sea journey, and even if I did not, it would be better so; at least you would know . . . there would be peace in the knowledge. Do not look so distressed. Long ago, Stephen Reynolds, whom I suppose we should now consider to be our good friend, told me I had a great spirit, and such is a source of strength.'

There might be truth in that, Andrea thought, and her mind dwelt longingly on the country which she had left as an infant, and the relations who were strangers to her, but who were prepared to make such efforts on her behalf. How wonderful it would be to say farewell to this stormy England and to Pleasance itself. Once she had been happy here, but now the estate had become an intolerable burden, and for all her courage she was nearly exhausted by her losing battle. House and grounds were becoming more derelict with every month that passed, and although there was money enough hidden away, she was in constant fear of the robbers and marauders who, having no connection with the Parliamentary forces, now roamed the ravaged country.

It was true that such as these would be summarily dealt with if apprehended. Cromwell had issued orders that death was the penalty for such ruffians who had frequently committed murders as well as robbery. Andrea had heard fearsome stories from time to time, but it seemed as though the villains were but rarely apprehended. Little wonder if to a girl not yet twenty-two who had suffered years of increasing anxiety, loneliness and sorrow, France seemed as desirable as the biblical promised land of milk and honey.

The three old servants who remained at Pleasance crept about like ghosts, unable to cope with more than the polishing and dusting of the few rooms which were now used, and leaving the cooking and the marketing to Andrea, who of all things detested the occasional necessity to show herself in the village, where she met with open hostility from those who grudgingly took her money, and who sometimes went so far as to call abusive words after her.

Andrea found it impossible to believe that the evil cloud which hung over the land would one day be dispelled. The calm, happy life had gone for ever, and for Lucy and herself there was only ruin and despair. More than all else she sorrowed over the vast, empty stables and the deserted paddock. She, herself, attended to the one horse which had been left behind; grooming him, keeping him in reasonable condition through solitary rides over the fields.

The parson and his family had long since departed, none knew where. The old Norman church had been despoiled and burnt and left a smoking ruin. Callers, with the exception of the faithful Dr Beale, were almost unknown. Those loyal to the King, if not driven from their homes, lived almost entirely within them where the doors were locked and the windows shuttered. They were afraid to move beyond, even to fraternize with the few of their kind within walking distance. Andrea realized that she was fortunate to have a horse to ride. In dozens of cases only useless coaches had been left to owners who were often elderly and infirm; incapable of road trudging.

One night, Andrea started up from her sleep at the sound of horse's hooves on the drive in which there were now pitfalls for an unwary rider.

She and Lucy usually retired early in the autumn and winter, to save light and fuel. It was not yet midnight according to the timepiece on Andrea's mantel, but even so who could be riding up the drive at this hour?

Throwing on a wrap, she unbolted the shutters at her window, and peered forth, but there were neither stars nor moon, and she could see nothing. Her heart was beating heavily, for no visit at this hour could bode them any good, or so she thought. When a summons came upon the locked and bolted massive outer door, it sounded oddly muffled and cautious, as though the one who wielded the knocker was wary of over-much noise.

This put some heart into Andrea, for one who came to rob would be unlikely to effect an entrance by lawful means. She slipped out of her room and as she did so a door farther along the passage opened, and Lucy appeared in gown and nightcap. If any of the old servants had heard the horse's hooves or the knocking on the door, they were evidently too frightened to stir.

'Should you open?' Lucy asked in a low, breathless voice.

'Yes, I think so. It could be someone in trouble . . . someone in flight,' Andrea answered.

Lucy, who had thought the same, uttered a sobbing moan. Would not this be bound to bring trouble upon them? But she did not protest. It was agreed between them, and had been from the first, that if one of their own kind sought sanctuary at Pleasance, they could not, at whatever cost to themselves, be turned away.

Andrea went down the long, curving stairs. With hands that trembled she shot back the heavy bolts and turned the key in the lock. Although she held a candle aloft, she could only see a few inches before her into the darkness, but then a rough though subdued voice said: 'Have no fear, Mistress. Stand aside and let me within. No harm will come to you.'

Lucy, from above, heard the voice and recognized it. She had followed Andrea, and by the time Stephen Reynolds had set the girl aside with a thrust of his elbow, Lucy was at her side. In his arms Stephen, muffled in a heavy cloak, was carrying an inert figure. Without a word, he laid his burden on the oaken settle in the hall.

Andrea glanced in bewilderment from the man to the one he had carried, but Stephen, paying no attention to her, looked at Lucy: 'We made a pact,' he said. 'I have kept my share of it, and I must fain call upon you to keep yours.'

Although now in his eighties Stephen looked less. He had broadened with the years and was a huge figure of a man, whose strength age had not yet enfeebled to any marked extent, though he was drawing his breath in heavy gasps, and his face was streaming with sweat.

'Who is it? Why have you brought him here?' asked Lucy, and crossing to the settle, she turned down a fold of the shrouding cloak.

Having glanced at the face it concealed, her gaze went back to Stephen. 'It is your son,' she said. 'The boy you drove away from home.'

'Aye, it's Ben,' assented Stephen heavily.

Andrea went quickly to the settle, and there was a moan and a restless movement as her hands moved swiftly over the prone figure. She said: 'He's wounded – bandaged! Has he had any attention from a surgeon?'

Stephen answered: 'More like one of his own men dressed the wound. I could not get a surgeon to him, though mayhap old Beale can be trusted to keep a still tongue in his head, if he's called in to him here. As I hoped to save Ben, I had to get him away from Derevale. It was only by the Lord's favour that I stumbled upon him in the dark. It would have been a different story had it been his brother Matthew or any of his men who for the nonce are quartered at Derevale. Word came that Rupert planned to set up the King's standard again in these parts, and had gathered together many of those who scattered at Marsden Moor. He thought to take us by surprise, but we, by the Lord's mercy were on the alert, and but yester e'en there was a skirmish with Rupert's men beyond Mellor, and many were put to the sword. Ben must have been one of them.'

'You should not have brought him here,' Lucy said tremulously. 'We would refuse sanctuary to none who fight for the King, even though if discovered it meant death to Andrea as well as to me; but your son is your responsibility, to shield, or to denounce, whichever seems good to you and your conscience.'

'Neither seems good to me,' groaned Stephen. 'Loyalty to the Lord's cause would bid me give him up; but loyalty to my own flesh and blood would bid me save him. His mother, poor soul, would be in agony could she know he was in such case as this. Where he hid before he managed to stumble homeward is not known to me, but of a certainty had he been in his right senses he would ne'er have thought of throwing himself on his brother's mercy seeing the hatred Matthew has for him, and the disgrace he is to our name. But Ben was in a delirium when I came upon him by chance, lying on the terrace steps. He opened his eyes to see me standing above him, and I was struck with amazement, for it was as though he was but a little lad, and had forgot all that had passed since then. He called me Father, and said he had done wrong to play truant, and would his mother forgive him as he had meant no harm . . .? What could I do, Lucy, but succour him? For hours, until it was black night, I hid him in a barn, but the danger of keeping him there was too great. In his fever he raved and sang and laughed, and every minute was a peril to him. If found, his life is forfeit.'

'Surely you exaggerate,' said Lucy coldly. 'It is well known that you have given much gold to help your cause. You also gave your two sons, one of whom you have lost. Would not this other son, even though he serves the King, be spared in consequence?'

'It would count for naught. Had Cromwell himself a renegade son he would not be spared,' Stephen retorted. 'Lucy, of your pity, do not refuse to shelter the lad. Once you had a kindness for him . . .'

'And still have,' said Andrea, before Lucy could speak. 'Of

course we will look after him. But first tell us, did you get him away from Derevale without being noticed?'

'To the best of my belief, I did. I waited until cover of darkness and then saddled a horse, and though 'twas an effort for a man of my age, I hoisted him upon it, and held him before me as I rode. None passed me on the way, and Matthew and his men were in the guard-room that has been set up at Derevale. He's as fine a preacher as he is a soldier, and tonight he was discoursing as I rode away.'

'You cannot have been suspected then, for eloquent though your godly son may be, I doubt not he would have set his brotherly blood-lust before his sermonizing,' Lucy observed sarcastically.

Stephen sighed heavily: 'There's the hard streak in you,' he said. 'You had it as a girl, but this young maid has a more tender heart.'

'That is true,' Lucy agreed. 'Wretched though the last years have been, Andrea has had less time in which to become hard. Fortunately for you, Stephen, she is of age and mistress here, and she has the right to say what shall be done and what shall not be done. You have heard her promise that your son shall be given our care. But where will be the safest to hide him? So far we have been immune, but...'

'And did I not send you a message that that was because of my pleas?' Stephen rapped out. 'It was I who said many a time and oft, that you had always been in secret sympathy with us and at one time would have been tokened to me, only that your folk came between us. I had the right to ask a favour, and as you had surrendered your livestock it was thought to be enough.'

'None the less, at any time your zealous friends may decide that here at Pleasance we have been shown too much forbearance. If the house were searched and Ben found here, if even a breath of suspicion fell upon us, we should receive short shrift.'

'The secret room, the priest's hole, where you once thought to put me, believing me to be dead, would not be discovered. It was of that I thought...'

For an instant Lucy pressed her hands against her tired eyes. Then she said: 'I had overlooked that, and Andrea knows nothing of it. I did not keep it from her by design, but because it had passed from my memory. She now sleeps in the room that was once mine.'

Andrea, who had been listening closely, demanded an explanation, and when she heard of the hidden room behind the panelling, she was amazed. How extraordinary that the memory of it should have passed from her great-aunt's mind. Such a room should be a safe refuge; that was to say if Lucy could remember how to open the secret panel.

She had not forgotten that, Lucy assured her. She had not actually forgotten the existence of the secret room. It had passed from her mind, she supposed, because there had never been occasion to use it. But even though there was such a refuge it would be difficult, if not impossible, to carry the helpless man up the long and winding staircase. Andrea had not the strength alone, and Stephen looked exhausted and would be unable to help her.

'I think with my aid he will walk, though but slowly,' said Andrea. 'His wound is through his shoulder and he has bled much and is weak, but if I entreat him – if I tell him he must do his best . . .'

Both the old man and the old woman watched her in wonder as she bent over Ben and spoke to him. She held his hands and murmured coaxingly, as she might have coaxed a sick child.

'You will do your best, will you not, Ben? It is for Andrea whom you protected long ago. See, I will lift you . . . you can sit upright, and with my help you can rise and put one foot before the other. There are not so many stairs to climb, and my arms will be round you all the time. It is for our safety, Ben, as well as yours.'

This murmuring voice continued for a few minutes, and then Lucy gasped as she saw the young man stagger to his feet. He looked, she thought with sudden pity, sick unto death. His eyes were wide open now and fever-bright, there was a deep flush on his cheeks; his lips were cracked and dry.

'If you would go ahead of us, Aunt Lucy,' Andrea begged. 'If you would open the panel door.'

Lucy moved quickly, as she had not moved for months, and Stephen followed behind Andrea, who with infinite patience coaxed the wounded man to ascend the stairs. Work in the stables and the garden had developed her natural strength, and she did not stagger under the weight of the only half-conscious Ben whose feet dragged and who moaned with the pain of the ascent.

The panelled door was open by the time they reached Andrea's room, and Lucy had taken spare candles from the chest where they were stored and put them on the table in the narrow, dark, little room. How long, how very long ago, thought Lucy, since she and her twin had played there; how long too since that eventful night which Stephen remembered.

'He must have a bed of some kind,' said Andrea, panting and flushed with the effort she had made. 'But that is easy. There are many that are unused in the rooms which have been locked up these many months. For tonight he shall have my mattress on the floor; tomorrow I will find a truckle bed. This room will hold it, if we take away the chairs.'

'The servants . . .?' warned Lucy.

'As they do not sleep in this wing they will notice nothing unusual. For months I have attended to my own room; they do not enter. Leave it all to me, and there will be no danger to any of us.'

Lucy had no choice, and after Stephen rode away from Pleasance, Andrea insisted that her great-aunt must go back to bed. She would make the wounded man as comfortable as she could, and on the morrow they would send Joseph for Dr Beale who could be trusted to keep their secret.

'Nursing will be required, and you know nothing of nursing,' said Lucy.

'I can learn, and Dr Beale will tell me what to do. Dear Aunt Lucy, pray don't look so perturbed. It is wonderful to be given an opportunity to help one who is for the King.'

'It will go hard with us if there is any suspicion and the hidden room is discovered,' said Lucy.

'How can it be, as only you until tonight knew of its existence?'

'Stephen Reynolds knew.'

'Nobody could be safer than he. His life would be in jeopardy . . . besides although he gave Ben such harsh treatment as a boy, he loved him. Even if Pleasance was ransacked, this room would not be found.'

Having at last persuaded Lucy to bed, Andrea had enough to keep her occupied for hours. She undressed Ben and eased his feverish body into a loose cotton smock, which she sometimes wore when gardening. She went down to the kitchen quarters and boiled water on a dying fire which she coaxed into a blaze. She filled a pitcher with milk, fresh that day from one of the few cows still left to them. In the cellar there were bottles of wine from a supply which had been laid down years ago. Andrea did not suppose that Ben, even if he recovered consciousness, would be able to eat, but she took a fresh-baked manchet and carried it with the warm milk and wine up the stairs to the room where he lay restlessly turning on the mattress she had taken from her own bed. This necessitated more than one journey, and she was thankful the three old servants slept at a distance.

Muslin kerchiefs of hers were torn into strips to make bandages, and having sponged Ben's fevered body she forced herself, though her hands trembled and she was fearful of causing fresh damage, to remove the blood-soaked pad on his shoulder to examine his wound.

Tears started to her eyes as she saw the deep, ugly gash, the torn flesh and muscles, but she was thankful too, for she was certain it had been caused by a sword thrust, not by a bullet, which might still be lodged in his flesh. And after all, she decided, she was not as inexperienced as her aunt supposed. Only a few weeks ago, one of the cats that lived in the deserted stables had been set upon by another and badly mauled. She had rescued the creature and had cleaned its wounds and it had recovered. That, with a half-wild and terrified animal had not been easy. Ben, on the contrary, was quiet beneath her gentle hands, and why should not the home-concocted salve which she had used for the injured animal be equally efficacious applied to a human being? In any case it could do no harm, thought Andrea, as she bathed and anointed and bandaged. Not ill-pleased with her handiwork, she was about to rise from her knees when Ben's eyes opened and he gazed at her, at first with perplexity, and then with pleased recognition.

'It's Andrea,' he said, 'and not a little wench any longer. What are you doing here, Andrea? Is it safe for you on the battlefield? Have a care, for there are scoundrels who drop upon the dead like vultures to rob them, and assault wives and sisters and sweethearts who come searching for their men. Marsden is far from Pleasance – and I was not wounded there – or was I? Was it a dream that I followed the Prince . . .?'

His rambling voice trailed off weakly, but the smile of pleasure still lingered. Andrea said softly : 'Don't ask any more questions – not yet. We are both safe, and all you need is to sleep and get strong again.'

She held a cup of milk to his parched lips, and he managed to drink some of it. He raised his hand and touched her cheek.

'Once it was bruised,' he said. 'You were a brave little wench. Be not too brave for your own safety. I would have you leave me, rather than imperil yourself.'

'Oh, hush !' Andrea murmured. 'It is all a dream, Ben. There is naught to fear . . .'

She held both his hands in hers, for it seemed to her that although he had a while back been far too hot, he was now alarmingly cold. She piled rugs upon him, but beneath them he shivered, and finally, she lay down beside him, drew his body close to the warmth of hers, pillowed his head upon her breast. Then he sighed with content, and presently he slept.

When Joseph was sent early the next morning to fetch Dr Beale, he asked no questions, supposing as had happened before that Lucy's state was giving some cause for concern. When the good doctor arrived and was furnished by Andrea with the sparse facts, he was ragingly angry. Attached as he was to both women and aware that Lucy's life-span could not be long prolonged, anxiety almost overwhelmed him when he contemplated the danger in which they were now involved.

So this was the fashion in which Stephen Reynolds demanded payment for the slight clemency that had been afforded them. An iniquitous bartering, Dr Beale fumed. The cowardly old man, afraid for his own skin if he harboured his son, had cast the burden upon them.

'I do not think he was exactly afraid,' said Andrea, 'but he saw the impossibility of hiding Ben at Derevale Manor, which from his account is now a garrison rather than a home. I am surprised that this is the first fugitive that has come our way. I won't pry into your secrets, but I have little doubt he is not the first whom you have been implored to secretly tend.'

'Aye, 'tis true enough.' The good doctor sighed. 'There have been such, hidden away in lofts and barns, and often discovered to be taken out and shot, even though there was but the bare breath of life in them.'

'Ben's hiding place won't be discovered. It is far better than any loft or barn,' said Andrea.

That was a fact which Dr Beale could not but admit when he was shown the secret chamber. He examined Ben's wound, praised Andrea for her care of it, assured her that he would bring her that day medicine and a salve which would both cleanse and heal, though the healing would take time, seeing that ligaments and muscles had been badly torn. Oh aye, he would recover, in answer to Andrea's anxious questioning. The fever would abate within twenty-four hours, but never again would he wield a sword with a strong right arm. There would be always a weakness, and probably some slight wasting.

'When he is in his right mind and questions you, do not tell him of it,' the doctor instructed. 'Not until he has recovered much of his lost strength, for it will be a blow to him. I make no doubt he is as bloodthirsty as most young men, and has a love of fighting for its own sake, let alone the King's cause.'

Anyone less bloodthirsty than Ben, as he lay there on the truckle bed which Andrea had contrived to pull into the little room, she could not imagine. He was of slight build, and looked scarcely more than a boy with his pale cheeks and closed eyes.

'It is your great-aunt for whom I most fear,' Dr Beale went on. 'I marvel that she has weathered the shock this must have been to her. See now that you do not allow her to rise from her bed today, and have a care of those cringing servants who stay on with you for their own purposes, because they are unwanted elsewhere. Even the dullest might suspect that something unusual is afoot, seeing that look in your eyes, my child.'

'What kind of a look? How can I help my looks?'

'You cannot,' Dr Beale agreed. 'It is nature working in you. You are a maid and he is a young man, not ill-looking, and the more certain of your tenderness because he is helpless and depends on you. Life came to a standstill with you when by rights it should have been your burgeoning hour; but now the hands of the clock have moved on again, and you are aware that you are a woman, a beautiful woman.'

Andrea laughed to cover an embarrassment that was strange to her. She turned away from the doctor's keen eyes to snuff the wick of a flickering candle, and remarked that it was as well old Joseph was on good terms with the chandler, for in this windowless chamber it would be necessary to keep a candle burning day and night. They would need to buy many, now they no longer made them as one of the household industries.

But her mind was not dwelling on this necessity; it had reverted to the long hours of the night before, when she had stretched out by Ben's side, striving to share the warmth of her body. His uninjured arm had fallen heavily across her; a knee had edged itself between her knees, a seeking hand had enclosed her breast.

There was no harm in it, Andrea thought defensively. He had not known, though he had turned to her for the animal comfort that she could give him. She had not wanted to move away, but had drowsed fitfully, with his hand still on her. When he had moaned and murmured, she had soothed him.

It would not happen again. The fever was passing, and tonight she would sleep in her own bed, though with the secret door ajar so that she might hear him if he called. There would be no danger of discovery, since her own bedroom door would be securely locked. As for the night that had passed, he would never know and she would forget. Sternly she repressed the thought that she did not want to forget.

CHAPTER 21

A secret life could be exciting, even though it necessitated constant care and the awareness of danger was never absent. Andrea discovered that during the next few days. She was buoyantly tireless and sustained by an unjustified optimism, for the future bristled with problems. Ben was improving, but who could say what would happen when he was well enough to leave his sanctuary? Andrea supposed that his father would devise some plan for his safety.

Stephen Reynolds had not been seen again at Pleasance, but Dr Beale had undertaken to report on his son's condition. Subsequently he told Andrea that Stephen had said he would provide aid when the time was ripe for it. Dr Beale had owned to feeling some pity for the old man who was, as he said, between the devil and the deep blue sea. Lucy retorted that that was no more than he deserved.

'He has suffered though,' said the more tolerant Andrea. 'His second son was killed, and for years he must have secretly worried about Ben.'

'He treated Ben cruelly when he was no more than a boy,' Lucy replied. 'I do not understand such love.'

Neither did Ben, who when he was in a rational state of mind and asked the inevitable questions, was amazed to be told that he had been brought to Pleasance by his father.

'Matt detests me,' Ben said. 'He always did, even when we were children, and as for my father, I should have expected him to hand me over straight away and to recite prayers as I was strung up on the nearest gibbet. Heaven alone knows what prompted me in my delirium to find my way to Derevale.'

'Your father must have always loved you,' said Andrea. 'He ran a great risk in hiding you and then bringing you here.'

'Which he should not have done . . . two women alone. If I were to be found . . .'

'But you won't be. Nobody except Dr Beale and your father

have any idea that this closet exists. You could stay here in safety for weeks or months, but of course it won't be for as long as that. Your father says he has a plan.'

Had she any notion, Ben asked, of how the war was going? With a downcast expression Andrea shook her head. Nobody seemed to know the King's exact whereabouts, though it was believed that Prince Rupert had got away to France.

'And then he'll be raising a fresh army to trounce the rebels,' said Ben, an admiring smile lighting up his face. 'Our Mad Cavalier, as the Roundheads call him, will never give up hope of victory. Though they may seem to be in power, he'll still find ways of tormenting them, and be sure of this, no matter how well they may be progressing now, that state is no more than an interlude.'

Andrea had heard Lucy and Dr Beale and others say the same thing, but it was hard to believe it, for in this part of the world there was a violent repudiation of royalty and all for which it stood. The bulk of the population had embraced Puritanism with an intense fervour. Singing, play-acting, dancing, were all discarded as snares of the devil; bright colours and trinkets were forbidden to women; drab browns and greys being the prevailing shades. Had it been possible, thought Andrea, the trees would have been robbed of their green and the flowers of their delicate beauty. She listened with fascination as Ben told her of the irrepressible Prince Rupert, handsome, courageous, and with a full quota of Stuart charm. Ben said proudly that early in the conflict he had been given the rank of lieutenant, and afterwards that of captain. He and his friend Philip Buxton had fought in one another's company, until Philip had been killed at Nazeby. The latest sortie in which Ben had been involved was a very minor affair, but it was the first time he had been wounded.

Of the actual encounter he could remember little, and of the fevered wandering which had ended on the terrace steps of his boyhood home, nothing whatsoever.

'I wondered if I should ever again see Pleasance,' Ben said. 'I've hated to think that as likely as not you and Mistress Grenton had been turned out and the place sacked. You say you have my father to thank for your safety, which is surprising.'

'I think he had a tenderness for Aunt Lucy long ago,' Andrea said. 'He spoke of it in my hearing, and she did not deny it. But something came between them, separated them.'

There was little space in the tiny room. Ben and Andrea sat side by side on the truckle bed. His shoulder was still bandaged, although the wound was healing fast, but his right arm had little strength in it and it was supported in a sling.

'It is singular,' Ben remarked thoughtfully, 'that there should have been this continuing association between our two families. It may be there was some link . . . some binding secret in the past. Andrea, I found a paper hidden away here . . . it was only yesterday.'

'Hidden?' Andrea glanced around the room. 'What hiding place could there be?'

'There's a drawer in the table, running the length of it. I pulled it out and there was the paper at the back. It must have been there for years.'

'Once this was a playroom for Aunt Lucy,' said Andrea. 'She and my grandfather used it for their games. They were twins, and he spent his childhood here with her, though afterwards his home was in France. Was there anything of importance written on the paper?'

'It must have been of importance to the people concerned. I did not show it to Mistress Grenton when she visited me yesterday to see how I fared. I thought it might convey more to her than to us . . . that it might be a reminder of something she would wish to forget.'

'What you mean is that Aunt Lucy could have hidden the paper here, and afterwards she forgot about it. Can I see it?'

Ben drew a sheet of thick, parchment paper from beneath the bed coverlet. It was covered with faded writing in the Italianate penmanship which, as Andrea knew, had once been fashionable. She bent forward to the candle-light to read it.

'I promise Susan Partridge that when I am the owner of Pleasance, I will give her a good cottage which shall be wholly hers. Also she shall have a fitting present when she is married, and after, for each year that she lives or that I live, there shall be given to her fifty gold pieces. And to this written promise I hereby sign my name, Annis

Grenton. In the year of Our Lord, One thousand, fifteen hundred and thirty-seven.'

Andrea read the words with a puzzled frown. The signature was written with a large, bold flourish. Even now it suggested a flamboyant defiance. The date was painstakingly printed.

'Annis Grenton was my great-great-grandmother,' said Andrea. 'This seems to have been a covenant between her and one Susan Partridge.'

'Partridge was the maiden name of my father's mother,' Ben said. 'One generation nearer to me because she was old, so I have heard, when she bore my father; and it was the same also in my case. I was the youngest, and my parents were both in middle-life.'

'Then,' said Andrea, 'my ancestress must have been much attached to your grandmother. It was a substantial provision to promise her, and she could have been no more than a girl when she made her promise.'

'There is more written on the other side of the paper.' And Ben turned it about to show her.

What was written there was evidently by a different person. The words were laboriously printed and ill-spelt.

'Ye take a tode, ye bigest to be found, and this ye well pric in plases, and put the tode in a covered jar, til it be dead and its juce has run out, then drane and store and mix with ye food or drinks, and who sups of it will fall sick and trubble ye no more.'

Andrea's colour faded as she read. She felt slightly sick and swallowed nervously. 'That—that is horrible,' she said.

'So I thought,' Ben agreed.

'It's as though there was an agreement between them—somebody was to be—to be poisoned, and then my great-great-grandmother was to reward the poisoner.'

'And the poisoner it seems was my father's mother.'

'I have heard Aunt Lucy say that your grandmother was personal maid to my ancestress and went with her to London when she was in attendance on Queen Jane, who was mother to King Edward, and died when he was born. They may

148

have been fond of each other at one time, but something hideous must have happened all those years ago between my ancestress and Susan Partridge. Oh Ben, I don't understand. If this paper fell into Aunt Lucy's possession, why did she not destroy it?'

'Who can tell? Sometimes one might be afraid to destroy a document, even though it seems incriminating. It might seem safer to hide it where only oneself could find it. With the passing of so many years your great-aunt's memory has faded, and it would not be well to show her this.'

'No – no, it would be a shock to her.'

Andrea's mind was driving back into the past, drawing upon all that Lucy had told her of those who had once owned Pleasance and had given it a devoted love. Annis Grenton, she remembered, had come into possession on the death of her father, but her stepmother was with child and had she produced a son, Annis would have been disinherited. Lady Grenton, however, had died before the child was born.

'There may have been some great wickedness,' said Andrea. 'But it is lost in time, and for that I am thankful. People have loved this house too well, loved it beyond pity or kindness.'

'Is it so with you?' he asked.

'No. My father, I am told, wished me to be brought up here, and he and my mother were bringing me home for that purpose when they were drowned at sea. Perhaps Pleasance might then have meant to my father what it has meant to Aunt Lucy; but to me it has always been a place I could leave if it were sensible for me to leave. I have no more than a moderate attachment, and have often thought I would prefer to live in France, from whence my mother's people came; and lately the sacrifice to preserve Pleasance has been too great.'

As she spoke, Andrea spread out her work-worn hands and gazed at them. She thought of all her heavy tasks, and the lack of friendship and companionship. Pleasance might have been compensation to Lucy, but not to her.

'I am supposed to be the image of that Annis Grenton who promised your grandmother so much,' she said. 'There is a painting of her in the picture gallery; not a very good painting, but it resembles me. She was fair and tall and strong as I am.'

'She could not have been so beautiful,' said Ben. 'Oh Andrea – my Andrea . . .'

His uninjured left arm was about her waist and she leant to him. Her heart was beating with a dizzy rapture. She had no doubt at all; all the doubt was on Ben's side; not of the depth of his love, but of his worthiness. 'Even as a child you were a wonder to me,' he said. 'I was heartsore to part from you.'

'But you only wrote once.'

'Oh, sweetheart, it was so useless! You were a child, but I was nearing manhood, and it seemed then that you could never be for me. Even now it seems so, for what have I to offer you? Not even a distinction I might as a soldier have won by Prince Rupert's favour. I shall never fight again with this near-useless arm.'

'There are other ways of fighting,' said Andrea. 'It is your plan, you said, to join the Prince wherever he may be, and he is not the one to reject you for wounds incurred in battle. He will find some use for you.'

'That was my own thought; that I could still be of service to him. But if he is indeed in France it may mean a long parting for us.'

'I doubt it. My relations in France have urged me to leave England, and have promised to provide the means. Aunt Lucy's weak health kept me here, but now she says she will take the risk of the journey. She insists she will be more likely to survive that than the separation from me; though indeed there could be none. I could never leave her.'

'For the life of me, I cannot see Mistress Grenton living happily anywhere but at Pleasance,' said Ben.

'It will be a terrible wrench for her,' Andrea said with a sigh. 'Oh, why has a house to mean so much? A guilding of stone and wood which may well outlast generations of human lives. There's a poison in that which I have escaped. All I want is to be with you, and it is there, whether in poverty or riches that I shall make my home.'

'Then nothing but death can separate us.'

Ben strained her close to him, and she smiled secretly,

securely, remembering that first night when he had clung to her, not knowing that he did. Some day perhaps she would tell him. Presently, when she could bear to move away from him, she took the old parchment sheet in her hand, and put one edge of it to the candle flame. They both watched as it slowly fell to ashes on the floor.

'That old wickedness was over long ago,' said Andrea, 'and none will ever know of it now. As for us, darling Ben, there shall be no secrets. This evening I shall tell Aunt Lucy that we love each other, and that for us a new life is beginning.'

✳ CHAPTER 22 ✳

Too old, too tired, too conscious of the shifting values of a changed world, Lucy did not protest overmuch when Andrea told her she was in love, and that as Ben had said, nothing save death could separate them.

'Oh, my darling, you have met so few,' said Lucy. 'You have been imprisoned here with only an old woman for company. How can you be sure that this belief of love is more than might spring up between any two young people thrown together in a romantic way?'

Andrea answered : 'Only my heart tells me it is more; that it is the great love which must come to nearly all people once in a lifetime.'

'It never came to me,' Lucy admitted. 'When I was still but a young girl I had an infatuation for your Ben's father, who was then very different from the man he afterwards became and is now. But it was not real, and before long I was glad to be done with him. There was too much to make it impossible, and I had Pleasance to fill my heart as I know it has never filled yours.'

'Is not that as well since I am bound to leave it? Ben, too, is set on getting to France, and soon should send a message to his father in the hope that he can help us. I have already gathered together all we most need, and our jewels and the money we have kept hidden.'

151

'Mayhap our enemies will permit the old servants to live on here for a while,' said Lucy, 'for it will soon be discovered that we have gone. We must leave money for their needs, and there is faithful old Joseph – but he is already provided for, and could have left us months ago but for the love he bears us.'

When Andrea saw Lucy to bed that night, the old woman took her glowing face in her hands and kissed her, saying : 'I want only your happiness, my darling, and so I shall tell your Ben. I have a liking for him, and he is, I doubt not, courageous and loyal. If he loves you better than all else, then the accident of birth is a poor thing in comparison. These are sad, hard times, and to one who will care for you, I give my utmost blessing.'

The tender words lingered in Andrea's mind and warmed her heart as downstairs in the kitchen she set about preparing the food which she would carry up to Ben. This was done late at night after the servants were abed, though when during the day she baked, and cooked meat and vegetables, she made sure there was more than enough for all. It did not occur to her that the greedy eyes of the old servants noticed the surplus of food. They talked amongst themselves of their young mistress's prodigious appetite, aware that pastries, and bread, and pitchers of milk which had been in the pantry late at night were no longer there by the morning.

Andrea would have been terrified had she known that eyes sharp as a rat's watched her through the chink of an almost closed door. Old Patty Shaw who had been in service at Pleasance since her girlhood, when Lucy too had been a girl, had crept from her room while her companions snored to spy upon Andrea, and now as she watched her, her toothless mouth fell open in astonishment.

All those locked rooms, thought Patty, and both the old mistress and the young so odd in their manner these last weeks. There could be only one explanation for that laden tray. Fugitives had been harboured in other houses not many miles away.

'The Lord has delivered mine enemy into the hands of his servant,' muttered Patty, certain that this, though perhaps in some slightly different form, came from the Good Book.

Lucy heard Andrea's footsteps as she ascended the stairs, and then the closing and locking of her door. She was always relieved when this last task of the day was accomplished. She supposed she should be thankful that Ben loved her darling, and would tenderly care for her. She should also be thankful that it would be no great grief to Andrea to live in a foreign land. For herself she dreaded it. There was not much life left in her, and what there was seemed to be so bound up in Pleasance that she doubted if it could still flicker within her when she turned her back upon the place. But that she must do, and soon, for Andrea's sake, who would not leave her here alone.

Sighing, Lucy raised herself in bed, pushed away the bed-clothes, and went over to the window. She folded back the shutters, and gazed out upon the gardens which tonight were bathed in moonlight.

The soft light was kind and accentuated the beauty, not the ruinous neglect. Lucy's gaze dwelt with an aching love upon the great trees and the spreading lawns – upon the terrace with its sundial and the mouldering statue of Ceres, the earth goddess, at the foot of the stone steps. She knew that her grandmother had commissioned a sculptor to produce this statue in order, so Annis had told her, to please her husband, Nicholas; though why it should have pleased him, Lucy had never fully understood.

She stood there by the window, while peace slowly stole over her. For so many years she had been part of Pleasance, as Pleasance had been part of her, and although she might depart from it, it seemed to her that something of herself would always be here.

Calm but weary, she at last turned away from the window and returned to her bed. As she pressed her cheek to the pillow and stretched her weary body, she had no prescience that the sleep now stealing over her was one from which she was fated not to awake.

Death came upon her without a dream, and when Andrea found her thus in the morning, she was smiling, and there was only the coldness of the cheek and hand Andrea touched to tell her that Lucy would never now be parted from Pleasance.

CHAPTER 23

A few days later, when Lucy was buried in the churchyard which surrounded the church that Puritan zeal had wrecked, there were only a few to stand around her grave.

Andrea and Dr Beale; a scattering of those who had been lifelong friends; old Joseph, who for the first time in living memory had tears in his eyes. Stephen Reynolds contrived to send a message, but he had not ventured to draw attention upon himself by joining the meagre funeral procession.

When the few mourners who returned to Pleasance with Andrea, where she dispensed a frugal hospitality, had left, old Joseph came to her and pushed a slip of paper into her hand. He said : 'I was to tell you, Mistress, to burn it when you had learnt the message by heart.'

Andrea did not read the message until she was with Ben in the room behind the panel, and then, having memorized what was written, the paper was burnt as that other sinister paper had been burnt.

'A ship at Harwich,' said Ben, 'which will put in there and stay for a few days, and the captain has instructions to receive two ladies as passengers, and to bear them across the sea to Holland. A brooch is to be shown him as a guarantee . . . a special brooch.'

'That was arranged long since,' said Andrea. 'My relations in France know of its existence, and instructed me to guard it well. The brooch is one which long ago was given to my great-great-grandmother by King Henry and Queen Jane.'

'And how do your French relations suppose you can get to Harwich?'

'They know I can ride, that I still have a horse. When Rebel, as he is called, was alone left to me, I exercised him and cared for him well. Sometimes I have been scared lest he might be taken from me, he is in such good shape. But I cannot follow these arrangements, Ben darling, unless your father can contrive your escape before then. I shall stay here with you, for how could you fare without me? You would be as badly off as though you were in a dungeon without food. My relations will try again for me later on.'

'A message must be sent to my father,' said Ben. 'He has promised to give aid, and that he must do, since he is responsible for my presence here.'

'Joseph could get word to him, I expect,' Andrea said. 'I will send him a message tomorrow.'

'My father may be here without a message. Mayhap he is already concerned with the proprieties, knowing we are left here together. It would certainly be so if he has taken my mother into his confidence, for she was ever of the belief that no man and maid could be left alone for an hour without moral catastrophe. It is thus that the Puritan mind works.'

'And yet your father was once so different. Aunt Lucy told me of how he was when he was young, and for many years afterwards.' ˙

'Which is why I raged at him as a boy, knowing from village gossip something of his past exploits. I called him a hypocrite for his psalm-singing. 'Tis small wonder that he thrashed me unmercifully. I don't hold that against him, but . . .'

'He repented,' said Andrea gently. 'Aunt Lucy could not bring herself to excuse him, but I was sorry for him when he brought you here; so torn as he was between his conscience and his love of you.'

It seemed that Ben understood his father, for that night when dark had fallen, a rider was once more heard approaching the house and Andrea admitted Stephen Reynolds. Nothing was said until Andrea had escorted him through her bedroom to the secret closet where Ben in full consciousness and for the first time in years was brought face to face with his father.

'Have a care there is nobody to overhear us,' said Stephen, 'for there is a traitor to you lodged within the house.'

Andrea stared at him in amazement. 'How can that be? There is nobody here at all, except the old servants and Joseph at the lodge. I could trust him with my life.'

'Him, maybe; but there is one at least of the old women you may not trust, one Patty Shaw. I was present today

when she came crawling to Matthew, to bleat out her suspicion that you had a fugitive here. It was her chance, with
you at the funeral. She had seen you preparing extra food,
carrying a tray up the stairs at night.'

Andrea was aghast. 'Oh, how could she? She and Aunt
Lucy were girls together. Patty wept when we found Aunt
Lucy dead. She said she was too upset to be at her funeral.'

'She said – she said – you are too simple, Mistress,' rapped
Stephen irately. 'The reward offered for sheltered fugitives
meant more to her than any mistress, alive or dead. See to it
that she is not around.'

Andrea searched the long passage beyond her room. At the
end of it there was a staircase leading to the servants' quarters
which generally stood open. Andrea locked it before she returned to Ben and Stephen.

'Did your son believe what Patty said?' she asked.

'He had his doubts, but tomorrow he'll be here with his
men to search the house, and I make no doubt to ransack it,
for he's been itching to get his hands on the treasures said
to be here.'

'None would find this hidden room,' said Andrea.

'That may be, but now there'll be a constant watch kept
on you, Mistress, and for that if for nothing else Ben must
be got away. I swore to Lucy that I would protect him, and
see that no harm came to you, and so I will, though how to
act is not yet clear to me. I had thought to leave Ben my
horse, and to see him on his way to the coast, where mayhap
he could lie in hiding for a while, and bribe some fishermen
or barge-owner. I have with me a uniform worn by one of
our men.'

Ben and Andrea exchanged a glance, and Andrea said
quickly : 'I have a better plan. There is a ship already at
Harwich, which was to take Aunt Lucy and me to Holland
and thence we should have journeyed overland to France.
Now there is no Aunt Lucy . . . only myself, but we had
clothes in readiness; a plain, dark gown and cloak, such as
your womenfolk wear, for Aunt Lucy, while I was to wear
man's apparel. We judged it safer that way, and less unusual
than for two women to be seen on the road alone. Now the
situation is different. Ben with his injured arm could scarce

ride your horse, but if he would agree – if he would not be too proud to wear a woman's garb and to ride pillion . . .'

She gazed pleadingly at her lover, who in spite of the extremity of the moment could not forbear a chuckle : 'If you think I could pass as a female, I will venture it,' he said. "Tis well I have no beard, and that you procured me a sharp razor, sweetheart.'

'I am certain you can pass,' Andrea said. 'You are very little taller than I, and with a hood and a muffling cloak who would suspect? As for horses, surely it would be better to take Rebel, not your father's steed, for if that were missing he would have to account for it. Also,' she added, suddenly tremulous, 'I have become fond of my poor horse, and would not leave him, perhaps to be ridden into battle and slain. Doubtless I could coax a place for him on board the ship.'

'Will the horse take you so far?' Stephen asked.

Andrea told him as she had told Ben that she was sure of it. The beast loved her, and without whip or spur, only the sound of her voice, he would put forth his best effort.

Stephen said : 'I have written out a safe conduct pass, and it will serve for two. It bears my son's signature and seal. A forgery, but a good one.'

'If things went wrong, might not your son deny all knowledge of it?' Andrea asked.

'No. In such a crisis, I should tell him what I had done, and Matt, who is a shrewd fellow, would see that I paid for it in solid gold : a more profitable retribution than for me to die a traitor's death. Two in the family would be more than he could stomach. It has been hard for him to own that he had a brother on the King's side, and months ago he gave out that Ben had been killed in battle. Matt would abet me for shame's sake.'

'We may never need to use the pass,' said Andrea. 'Myself, I think it unlikely we shall be challenged for we shall be riding through the night; a merchant, a native of Harwich who has journeyed inland to escort his wife home after a visit paid in these parts.'

Stephen asked : 'Even if poor Lucy's heart had been stronger, I doubt that she could have survived such a journey.'

Tears shone in Andrea's eyes. 'We determined to risk it,

because we thought it less of an agony than that she should be left behind. The plan we had was different. I would then have been her son, and she my sick grandmother, fain whatever the consequences to return to her family home. I have tried on the clothes and make a passable young man. I am tall and strong, my hands are not small, idle woman's hands . . .'

'You would do better to wear the uniform I purloined,' Stephen said. 'It is girt with a sword belt. If Ben is not affronted at wearing woman's apparel, you, Mistress, can also crush your Royalist pride and act the Puritan.'

'I would act the devil himself, sport his hooves and horns, were it to be an advantage,' Andrea said impatiently. 'It might be, too, if I rode into a band of roisterers. Such an apparition would send them flying.'

Stephen grinned at her, liking her the better for her spirited impudence. 'There's no time to lose,' he said. 'The clothes are in my saddle-bag. Get them and see if they will make a passable disguise. You will have to cut your hair, my lass. I vow that when unbound, it must fall past your waist.'

Ben bitterly regretted this, and said so, but to Andrea it was unimportant. She had always known that her ringlets must be sacrificed. They would grow again. In the end it was Stephen who trimmed the raggedly shorn locks, and planted the plain Puritan's hat upon them. It was he, also, who helped his son into the dark woman's dress and hooded cloak.

Stephen handed over the formal safe conduct pass, and at the last minute, after Andrea had gone round to the stables to saddle Rebel and to lead him round to the front of the house, the old man drew out a sheepskin bag and gave it to his son.

'You have had nought from me for many years,' he said gruffly, 'and will have no portion in such as I can leave, which provides for your mother and for Matthew. This is in lieu of all you saw fit to forfeit.' And then as Ben hesitated, he said: 'Take it, and be off with you, and may the Lord bless you and have you in His keeping.'

There were tears in his eyes, and roughly embracing Ben

he helped him to mount behind Andrea who was already in the saddle.

'Somehow, when we are safely away, we will get word to you, Father,' said Ben, himself not unmoved.

The moon came out from behind clouds, and Stephen stood by his horse waiting to watch them ride away before starting off in the opposite direction.

Andrea, as she rode down the drive, with the comforting pressure of Ben's arm about her waist, turned for one last glance at Pleasance, bland and gracious in the moonlight. It was unlikely that she would ever see it again, but she felt no deep regret, though for an instant she saw it as in the days of her childhood. Almost she could have imagined that the shadow thrown upon the terrace by the moving boughs of the nearest tree was the shadow cast by the slender, graceful form of Lucy, who had so often stood there to welcome Andrea when after a canter through the meadows she rode up the drive towards her.

Now as she turned away from that which in memory had become the beloved Lucy's shrine, Andrea raised her hand in salute.

Hours later (and what long and anxious hours they seemed in retrospect) Ben and Andrea stood side by side on the deck of the Dutch ship, which after unnerving delay had at last set sail.

There were few passengers, and most of these, so Andrea guessed, were those to whom it had seemed but wisdom to desert their native land. She had seen many faces as white and strained as her own must be, and had heard more than one sob of relief as the ship sailed out of harbour.

There had been a few moments of laughter as, in the shelter of a cramped cabin, they had changed their clothing. It was a profound relief to Ben to be wearing a man's garb again, even though it was that of an officer in Cromwell's army. His own torn and bloodstained garments had been left in the secret closet and Andrea had nothing but the sombre gown and cloak which had been his disguise on leaving Pleasance; but she fastened at her throat the Queen's brooch, which was now more than ever an heirloom to be treasured.

Ben promised himself that a suit entirely unlike the Puritan uniform would be the first thing he would buy with his father's gold, while as for Andrea, what joy to see her in glowing silks. With a sigh for her sacrificed ringlets, he drew his hand caressingly over her shorn head, and Andrea who was pleased with her short, clustering curls, smiled at him.

'What matter,' she said softly; 'the bad times are over now – for us. It is happiness and being together that lies ahead.'

'And no regrets?'

'The word has no meaning for me,' she said, and meant it.